SHINE HOUSE

An Emmie Rose Haunted Mystery Book 0

A PREQUEL NOVELLA

DEAN RASMUSSEN

Shine House: An Emmie Rose Haunted Mystery Book 0: A Prequel Novella

Dean Rasmussen

For more information about this book, visit:

www.deanrasmussen.com
dean@deanrasmussen.com

Shine House: An Emmie Rose Haunted Mystery Book 0: A Prequel Novella

Published by: Dark Venture Press

Cover Art: Mibl Art

Developmental & Line Editor: C.B. Moore

❧ Created with Vellum

It was an offer Emmie couldn't refuse. An invitation to spend her spring break vacation at her friend Angela's house near Cypress Harbor in Northern California. She had seen the pictures. The house was set high on a cliff surrounded by forest and fields overlooking the ocean, far from the heavy traffic and incessant noise of Los Angeles. It might be her best chance to find some solitude away from her past—away from all the death.

But now, as her friend drove them to her home, Emmie had that familiar sinking feeling in her chest. The sensation that something awful had happened just ahead. It gnawed at her stomach, and only a few minutes later, the traffic slowed to a crawl.

A frenzy of blue, white, and red lights flashed over the cars in front of them. Several police cars had blocked off both lanes, diverting the traffic to the shoulder on the far right. A firetruck, a rescue unit, and some ambulances blocked the view as they approached.

Emmie's heart beat a little faster while she clenched her hands into fists, although her growing anxiety was a far cry from the panic attacks she'd endured as a child. She'd come a long way since then, now able to control her "gift" with the help of techniques she'd practiced almost daily. But the presence of death was impossible to ignore.

Despite her chill, she straightened in her seat. She wasn't afraid. Not anymore. And Angela couldn't know anything about Emmie's past. It was better that way.

"Oh, I hope they're all right," Angela said as they approached the scene.

Emmie kept her eyes forward but picked out the details from the edge of her peripheral vision. No sense in looking at it directly. "I'm sure they are."

Angela craned her neck as they passed the wreckage a moment later. "Oh, no..." she said sadly. "A family."

Emmie swallowed hard. Of course, her "sight" had once again proven true, and she already knew the outcome. But she resolutely fixed her gaze on the police officers as they directed the traffic away from the mangled cars. It was better to focus on the living at moments like those. Less of a chance she'd see one of *them*. And she hadn't seen one of them for months now.

Knock on wood.

She had trained herself to tune them out, and had become quite good at it, unless... unless they caught her off guard. And sometimes they did, slipping through and approaching her when she least expected it.

She shivered.

Angela glanced over. "Cold?" She reached for the AC and turned it down a bit.

Emmie shrugged it off and forced a smile. "Not at all."

The last thing Emmie wanted was for Angela to think there was something odd about her. Angela's friendship had come at a time when Emmie wondered if anyone would ever get close to her again. This was a chance to finally start over and connect with a reality she had never known—to have a *real* life.

"You will," Angela said. "It gets chilly near the ocean, but it won't matter after you see the view."

Something over Angela's shoulder caught Emmie's eye, and

she instinctively stared at it. A pink backpack lying on the side of the road. A child's backpack.

Emmie looked away sharply. Focusing for too long on it would attract *their* attention. She closed her eyes for a moment, pushing her eyelids together as if to erase all that she'd seen, then opened them again. She had gotten good at tuning them out.

Her friend clutched the steering wheel tighter, while straining higher again in her seat to get a better view. "Four ambulances. That can't be good."

Allowing herself to look again, Emmie focused on one car with its top crushed as it lay on its side. Judging from the twisted wreckage, it was unlikely that anyone inside had survived.

The two other vehicles were even worse, nearly torn in half, with broken glass and blood splattered in every direction. A white van and an SUV. The van had pushed in the front end of the SUV so far that the front bumper sat where the driver's gas pedal would have been. There were papers and a torn shirt on the ground beside one window, and the smell of gasoline filled the air. A glint of light reflected off a shiny surface: a cellphone lying in the grass.

Through the open and shattered window of the van, Emmie spotted a woman lying motionless in the wreckage, her body draped over one of the rear seats. Three firefighters were attempting to pry the van's door open from the other side while more EMTs shuttled a small body covered with a white sheet on a gurney to a waiting ambulance.

The heartbreaking scene took Emmie's breath away, and she returned her focus to the cars in line ahead of them. At least, she hadn't seen any spirits, but she wouldn't see the adults anyway— she could only see the spirits of children. A torturous "gift" she had worked so hard to crush in recent years, though moments such as this certainly tested her confidence.

An officer ahead with a stern face shouted and made wide gestures at the side of the highway, urging each car to hurry along without gawking. He singled out Angela, his face growing red as he shouted more loudly, but she didn't seem to notice.

She was still staring at the carnage. "Looks like the van must have crossed over the center median and flipped over."

After they'd passed the accident, Angela glanced over with a reassuring smile and touched Emmie's hand. "I guess tragedies remind us of how fragile life is."

Her friend was only trying to comfort her, but the awareness of death still lingered long after they'd passed. Emmie nodded while trying to put on a brave face. "I could use a few less reminders."

"We're almost there." Angela sped faster down a two-lane road with only the occasional home flashing past the windows.

The clean, salty smell of the ocean hung in the air. Emmie couldn't see the ocean yet, although she peered as far as she could through the trees. The hills rose and fell as they approached their destination, like a gentle roller coaster sending the same sort of butterflies through her stomach.

Would it really be as wonderful as Angela had described? Her friend had certainly hyped up the experience as if Emmie might turn down the opportunity. No way. No chance of that. But Emmie tempered her expectations. Despite the isolation, it was foolish to think she could ever get away from *all* of them.

The ocean wasn't the draw—she could do that anytime simply by driving an hour from her dorm room at Catalina Crest College over to Redondo Beach or any of the other sprawling beaches on the Los Angeles coastline. She could see it any time, but this was somehow different. It was her chance to *truly* enjoy it without the tourists or crowds or... the victims.

Her heart was beating faster again. The anxiety threatened to derail the joy, so she took a deep breath and pushed the thought away.

Clear your mind, Em. You're on vacation. Remember?

She shook her head almost imperceptibly and meditated for a few seconds. The chatter in her head melted away and her breathing slowed to a deep and steady rhythm.

Angela suddenly pointed ahead. "There it is!" A red, white and blue painted mailbox rose above a patch of flowers at the corner of a narrow driveway, although trees obscured any view of the property.

A thin, silvery mist permeated the air. It filled the ditches beside the road and stretched across the floor of the forest around them. The sunlight almost seemed to sparkle within the cottony air, giving the impression that they were driving among the clouds.

"Can't help the fog," Angela said as she turned into the driveway. "It's like that most of the time up here."

"It's heavenly," Emmie said.

Angela laughed. "You'd change your mind if you lived here. Half the time you can't see the road. Accidents all the time."

Turning into the driveway a moment later, the white, two-story house came into view. It was off to the left with a view of the ocean straight ahead. The light fog hung over the water too, although it only added to the breathtaking view. The cloudless blue sky mirrored the water's surface, and except for some ships and smaller sailboats in the distance, the scenic tranquility was invigorating. Perfect, so far.

Angela came to a stop behind three other cars parked beside the house and threw her driver's door open as soon as she turned off the engine. "Finally."

Emmie did the same, climbing out and standing with her friend in front of the car for a moment as the smell of pine trees, ocean, and clean air filled her lungs. It was a stark contrast to the prevalent smog of Los Angeles. Angela had hyped up the location as an oasis by the sea.

A perfect description for this slice of paradise. Even better than she could have imagined.

Moments later, a tall burly man stepped toward them from around the house wearing a red flannel shirt with his sleeves rolled up. Adjusting his baseball cap embroidered with a black, white and blue US flag across the front, he scratched along the edge of his light brown crew cut hair and grinned at Angela as she charged toward him.

"Papa!" Angela said to him.

The man's expression brightened as Angela hugged and kissed him, towing him toward Emmie while keeping her arm around him as if to prevent him from running away. Angela pushed her dad to an uncomfortably close distance in front of Emmie. "Dad, this is Emmie."

The burly man stepped forward and wiped his hand on his pants before holding it out. "Marty."

They shook hands, and his grip startled her—it was a little too firm. But Angela had said her dad was a former cop, so he was probably used to displaying firmness in his encounters. She let go and nursed her aching hand silently.

"If you need anything..." Marty continued.

Emmie rubbed the muscles between her fingers but smiled. The pain wouldn't take away from the joy she felt now at all the beauty around her.

Still clinging to her father, Angela snatched his baseball cap and buzzed her fingers over the top of his head. "Dad still thinks he's in the Marines."

Marty grabbed his hat back and slipped it on. "I like it like this."

"You should let it grow out."

"Like yours? No chance." He grimaced. "You're a spitting image of Rapunzel. Get my scissors."

Angela pulled away as if he might actually go through with it and laughed while stroking her long hair. "No chance."

Meeting Emmie's gaze, Marty grew silent for a moment as if

he were studying her, until Angela tugged his arm while handing him the keys to the car.

He smirked, glancing down at the keys in his hand. "So I'm playing valet too?"

"I'm on vacation." Angela grabbed Emmie's arm and towed her toward the house in the same way she'd done to her dad moments earlier.

Emmie glanced around the area while approaching the house, then back at the car. Marty was already lifting both their suitcases from the trunk, but he seemed not to mind.

Angela yanked her along. "You won't believe the view."

Circling the house, they met a grassy lawn that stretched out toward the edge of a rocky cliff. To the left was a massive fire pit with several white wooden lawn chairs circling a pile of scrap wood stacked five feet high, and beyond that was a neatly manicured garden filled with vibrant flowers of all colors. A forest circled the property like a veil. To the right, the light mist shimmered in the sunshine, but the edges of the cliff jutted from the haze as the ocean waves crashed against the shoreline somewhere out of sight below.

Pausing only a moment to take in the view, Angela yanked her toward the house. A white swing on the porch swayed gently in the light breeze and a cluster of potted green plants sat beside the entrance. Stepping over a well-worn welcome mat, Angela led Emmie into the house.

A warmth filled her as soon as they stepped inside. The cozy surroundings reminded her of... family. A certain holiness that she had longed to find after escaping her home in Minnesota right after graduating from high school. The place held a strength and a safety.

Angela seemed to pick up on her feelings, watching with a curious smile. "Beats a college dorm room, right?"

"Definitely."

"And I'm saving the best for last." Angela grabbed Emmie's

hand again and led her further into the house. Passing another group of framed photos taken when Angela must have been a preteen, they passed a wall near the dining room that displayed a few awards for her parents' military service. The thick black frames stood out against the soft beige walls. Beside that, another finely crafted wooden display held an assortment of medals and a US flag folded into a triangle at the bottom of the case so that only the stars of the flag showed.

Emmie passed her eyes over Angela's fit body. It made sense now. She had inherited her parents' healthy traits and habits.

They walked up a flight of stairs and continued down a short hallway with doors on both sides, then turned into a bedroom at the end. Light poured in through three large windows straight ahead. The walls were painted a subtle blush pink and a white plush comforter covered a queen mattress that took up most of the room. A mosaic of framed photos filled the top of a tall dresser and a cluttered computer desk sat in the corner.

But the spectacular view of the ocean took Emmie's breath away.

"This is where you'll be staying," Angela said. "It's my room —at least it's still my room on weekends—but I'll sleep in the guest room. Only the best for my friend."

Emmie met Angela's gaze. "I—"

Angela held up her hand with a grin. "Don't argue. I need something to drink. Don't you?"

Before Emmie could answer, Angela was leading her back downstairs toward the kitchen, and they passed the living room along the way. A massive stone fireplace crackled with dancing flames, and the black screen of a large TV mirrored their silhouettes as they came between it and the massive bay windows behind them that looked out over the ocean. A mix of plush leather sofas and armchairs were neatly arranged around a glass coffee table. There were bookshelves but not many books. Instead, the shelves were filled with other decorative items like vases and sculptures and antique items resembling family heirlooms.

Emmie took a moment to look at some of the photos against one wall. Angela's family huddled and smiling in front of the Grand Canyon, and another showed Marty dancing in a sleek suit jacket with a woman in a ruffled red dress with a "Tango Championship" banner draped across the wall behind them.

Emmie gestured at the woman. "Your mom?"

"They were both stationed in Sacramento when they met. I'm sure they pray every night that I'll follow in their footsteps, but... I doubt it. Having too much fun right now."

"What kind of fun?" Marty's voice came from behind them as he walked in the front door and set the suitcases in the living room. "I better not get any calls from my buddies down south."

"You're just bringing those in now?" Angela scoffed with a grin.

"Busy on the phone. Flavio and Red are heading over with the truck to drop off another load of wood for the bonfire."

"Oh?" Angela's face lit up while looking at Emmie. "You'll like meeting Flavio..."

Marty rolled his eyes. "Don't start trouble, Angie."

"*Angela*, thank you very much." She frowned. "I'm not ten anymore."

"Angela," Marty corrected himself. "Sometimes I forget." He winked at her, then grinned at Emmie for a moment before walking outside.

"Who's Flavio?" Emmie asked after Marty left.

Angela's eyes narrowed and her grin spread wider. "A young cop who used to work with Dad. *You'll* see."

Leaning back, Emmie folded her arms over her chest. "Should I be afraid?"

Angela laughed. "Oh, yes. Be very afraid. No, relax. He's a sweetheart." She led Emmie over to the front door and they stepped out into the sunshine and breeze. Angela made a wide gesture toward the ocean and spoke loudly. "No worries at all. Isn't it great?"

"Perfect."

Angela held up a hand. "Oh, I forgot something. Wait here."

A moment later, Emmie was alone as a cool breeze swept in from the ocean, ruffling her hair and clothes, and the sunshine warmed her face. It reminded her of an early summer afternoon in Minnesota by the lake. With her eyes closed, the ocean's energy seemed to lull her until a group of birds broke into flight from a nearby tree.

Angela returned almost at the same time carrying two full glasses of a yellow drink mixed with ice. She handed one to Emmie.

"Alcohol?" Emmie asked.

"Too early. Lemonade."

As they walked out toward the fire pit, Emmie scrutinized the wood scraps piled at its center. The rotten and broken pieces of wood seemed far out of place among the scenic beauty of the ocean as a backdrop. The pile was a mix of discarded furniture, floorboards, door frames, window frames, scrap wood and a few dead tree branches. It all sat within a circle of bare sand surrounded by an ankle-high wall of bricks that was charred on the side facing the middle.

"What's going on there?" Emmie gestured to the pile.

"For the bonfire," Angela said. "They've still got a few days to build it up before Red lights it on Friday. It'll be spectacular. I can't wait."

Emmie studied the chaotic pile. Maybe a structure had collapsed in an earthquake, or someone had renovated an old house? "Where did it all come from?"

Angela's expression turned solemn. "Next door."

Only a moment later, a woman approached them wearing a wide-brimmed straw hat, sturdy boots, soiled garden gloves and a long-sleeved shirt smeared with dirt and grass stains. She had a steely stare with a no-nonsense demeanor. A garden apron hung around her waist, but she removed it, along with the gloves as she approached.

"Hi, Mom." Angela hurried forward and embraced her mother.

Emmie stayed back to give them some privacy. The woman's arms stretched around her daughter, revealing a tattoo of the word 'Relentless' along her left arm beside a hawk caught in a dive.

After a few seconds, Angela brought her mother over, stopping her in front of Emmie.

They shook hands, introducing herself as Kelsey. The woman had the same firm grip as her husband. She wiped her forehead with the back of her hand while looking toward the wood pile. "We've never had a bonfire on our property before. It'll be interesting to see what happens." She glanced toward the trees in the area. "Have you ever been to one?"

Emmie nodded once. "Many years ago."

"We'll keep a close eye on it. No fire restrictions at the moment, and it should be fun." Kelsey glanced at their drinks, then looked back toward the front door. "I should get cleaned up. Red and the others will be here soon."

"We'll be here."

Looking toward the ocean, then out over the tops of the trees, Emmie spotted some sort of tower rising above them. Angela *had* mentioned a lighthouse nearby... Was that it? It was so close, but only the glassy tower of its top was visible from that angle. "The lighthouse?"

Angela followed her gaze. "That's it. On the neighbor's property."

"I thought you didn't have any neighbors."

"Nobody lives there... anymore. And it won't be around much longer."

"Why is that?"

Angela's expression softened. "Nobody wants to buy it after what happened to the Davidson family nine years ago..."

Emmie tensed, although her friend had trailed off without elaborating. But still, she couldn't help but imagine what had happened to the family nine years ago. No doubt, a murder or suicide or some other horrible tragedy. Something unspeakable that had left behind troubled spirits. And they would try to make contact with her, as they always did in one way or another.

It was exactly what she didn't want to hear. The tranquility she'd embraced since arriving had vanished in an instant, and even though she'd managed to deal with her gift since arriving in California, the unexpected discovery was a harsh reminder that she could never truly escape her twisted reality, not even for a single, blissful week of vacation. They were always there.

Pushing aside her fear, Emmie couldn't ignore that her friend's eyes were watering with a deep pain. Reaching out, she took Angela's hand while avoiding even a glance toward the lighthouse again. "I'm so sorry."

Angela nodded slowly. "It was a shock to everyone."

"I can't even imagine."

Angela gestured to the pile of wood. "It's better this way. Red and Flavio are grabbing whatever scraps of wood they can from what's left. Red does architectural salvage, so he's trying to save as much as he can to sell or recycle. And whatever he can't use, we'll burn."

"Can't they renovate it instead of tearing it down?"

"It's too far gone to restore. But Red's on the City Council, so he wouldn't let anything worth saving slip away."

A moment later, a truck loaded with scrap wood pulled into the driveway and backed across the yard, stopping a few feet from the edge of the fire pit. Two men stepped out. A balding, middle-aged man and a younger, black-haired man. Emmie's gaze immediately locked onto the young guy. He wore jeans and a plain white T-shirt that hugged his healthy body with a flannel shirt tied around his waist. Dirt and specks of sawdust dotted him from head to toe. He held a confident demeanor as he started unloading the truck with a mesmerizing grace.

Angela beamed at Emmie. "You like?"

Emmie's face warmed again. She sucked in the rest of her lemonade, licked her lips, and handed her glass back to Angela with a grin. "I'm going to need something stronger."

❧ 3 ❧

Emmie tried not to stare. Flavio glanced over at her once, and his warm smile was a stark contrast to every other encounter she'd ever had with a cop.

Angela took Emmie's glass of lemonade with a cheeky grin. "Keep an eye on things." Angela winked, then walked back into the house with their glasses.

Flavio and Red started unloading the back of the truck without glancing over at Emmie. Flavio seemed to effortlessly jump into the cargo bed and started passing the scraps of wood to Red, some of them as large as the cargo bed itself. Working in unison, they emptied the truck within a few minutes and the bonfire heap grew another several inches. Even with the cool breeze coming in off the ocean, Flavio's skin shone with a light sweat. There was a lightness in the way he moved, a gracefulness that could only come from a focus on strength and fitness, although he wasn't excessively muscular.

"Let them break their backs."

A woman's voice had come from beside Emmie, breaking her out of her semi-trance.

Emmie glanced over and met the woman's gaze. She was tall with a soft, mischievous smile, with blond hair that stopped just short of touching her earthy green sweater. She had earrings made from raw crystals and a string of several tiny seashells strung through her necklace.

"You're Emmie." The woman extended her hand, her bracelets jingling softly—the largest piece was silver and resembled a series of interconnected feathers.

Emmie shook her hand and nodded. "That's me."

"I'm Sherry, Red's wife." Sherry glanced back toward the woodpile. "It's such a shame we couldn't have saved more. But when the elements get to it, there's only so much we can do."

Emmie glanced toward the lighthouse tower, although she could only see the tip from where she stood. "It's falling apart?"

"Rotting from the inside. After the roof collapsed, there were too many leaks... so much damage. We managed to save some of it—much to the delight of my husband—but the rest will get recycled into the wind, I'm afraid."

Emmie turned back to Flavio as he picked up a few scraps from the grass and tossed them into the pile.

Sherry gestured to the wooden chairs that circled the fire pit. "I have to sit down—the arthritis in my knees is acting up again. Care to join me?"

Emmie did, following the woman to a couple of chairs that faced the ocean with the lighthouse—and Flavio—to their right within Emmie's peripheral vision.

Only a minute later, Red stepped over carrying a towel and sat down beside Sherry. He removed his gloves, dropped them on the ground at his feet, and leaned back against the chair while letting out a sigh of relief. "Insanity."

"What's insane?" Sherry asked him.

"So much work for such a little reward."

"It's a labor of love."

"And insanity," Red added.

"But you love it, don't you?"

He grinned. "I do."

Sherry introduced Red to Emmie, but he made no effort to reach out to her.

"I'd shake your hand," he said, holding up his sweaty palms, "but you wouldn't like me afterwards."

Emmie inched back. "It's totally all right. I understand."

Red wiped his hands on the towel he'd carried with him, then swiped it over his bare head. "Sorry about the glare. Had a full head of ginger back in my day, but then I had kids."

Sherry laughed. "Don't blame them."

He scoffed. "And a wife."

Sherry smirked and turned to Emmie. "Don't listen to him. This is how he gets after a day of architectural salvage. All wound up, like coming home with a trophy after a day's hunting."

Red nodded. "True."

Emmie glanced toward the lighthouse again. "What happens to the pieces of the house that you're not going to burn?"

"Sell it," Red said. "Not much money in my hobby, at the end of the day, but to me it's like digging up lost treasure."

Sherry frowned. "We have two garages full of his *treasure*. No more room, but he keeps bringing it home."

He grinned. "You've never complained before."

"When have I *stopped* complaining?"

"It's worthwhile."

"Yes." Sherry seemed to relax.

"The architecture was so beautiful back then, wasn't it?" Red laughed. "Neither of us can let it go to waste. I guess we're both hoarders, to a degree. And the stories of bootleggers are irresistible. They used to land along the shore during prohibition, you know? The gentle slope of the shore made it easy for them to get from the beach up to the lighthouse. They used to shuttle in moonshine all the time in the 20s, which is where the name 'Shine House' came from. I remember reading that someone even found a trove of silver coins hidden in one of the caves down there. I'm sure it's all gone now, but they used the caves to do their business. Don't think the cops ever caught on to this one, anyway. They flew under the radar, for the most part."

Emmie craned her head around to get a peek at Flavio but caught sight of the lighthouse tower instead. The sunlight pierced through broken windows and jagged frames, exposing a darkened interior, although she could see a few small details from that distance. The massive light at its core used to warn approaching ships and a shadow beside it. Clouds passed over them, blocking the sunlight and chilling the air further. Emmie blinked, and the shadow was gone.

Emmie shivered and looked away. A trick of light?

But Red had followed Emmie's gaze toward the lighthouse. "Have you heard of Shine House, by any chance?"

"Angela told me some of it."

He seemed to study her face, then nodded solemnly. "I see. Yes, lots of history in that place, that's for sure, and none of it good. Not the topic of choice around here in recent years. You can't see much of it from here, but there's a small house attached to the lighthouse where the Davidson family used to live. They were renovating the place, fixing it up all nice, and started on the lighthouse with the intention of making it a tourist attraction, but I guess the lure of the old smuggling stories attracted the wrong type of people. Someone broke in one afternoon and murdered the whole family."

A silence passed between them. The sun came out from behind a cloud, but a chill spread through Emmie's body. The horrific event was even more awful than she'd imagined. But the property sat behind a group of trees, and she had no reason to go over there, so it wasn't the end of the world. She could manage the discovery, just as she had always managed, but it would always sit at the edge of her awareness.

Flavio broke the tension a moment later after he stepped over with a towel and wiped the sweat from his face while introducing himself to her. "Flavio Oliveira."

She stood and shook his hand, ignoring his sweaty palms. "Emmie Fisher, Angela's friend."

"Emmie," he repeated, gesturing to the wood pile. "Ever been to a bonfire?"

"Never."

He nodded. "Perfect. This one will light up the night sky."

"It won't get *that* bright, will it?" Sherry asked.

"Lots to burn." Flavio draped the towel over the armrest as he sat down, leaving one chair empty between them. He pointed to the seat. "I better save a spot for Angela."

Emmie smiled. She wanted to say something to him, anything really, just to break the ice. Words hung at the tip of her tongue, but she couldn't get "the murders" out of her mind.

It didn't help when Flavio glanced back toward the lighthouse. "We should have it all cleared out soon. And it's high time..." A serious look formed on his face.

Sherry leaned into Emmie and lowered her voice while glancing toward the lighthouse. "The murders were a shock for the whole town. You know, nothing ever happens out here, so far from the city. Nothing *that* violent, anyway. Angela's father and his partner found the bodies a few days after it happened."

Flavio looked at Emmie. "I was just a kid at the time. It spooked the hell out of everyone, especially after what happened to Lily." He studied her curiously for a moment, then leaned toward her. "Did Angela say anything about Lily?"

Emmie forced a smile and shook her head, while wrapping her arms over her chest. "No."

"We don't need to go through the details." Sherry reached over and touched her arm. "It was a long time ago."

Over Flavio's shoulder, Emmie couldn't help but see the lighthouse from the corner of her eye, but she refused to turn her head in that direction. "I'm fine."

"It shocked all of—" Flavio stopped.

The door to the house creaked open and the conversation

ended. Angela had stepped out of the house holding a tray of glasses. "Who needs a drink?"

"I do," Emmie burst out.

Flavio stared back at her with an amused expression, then stood and hurried over to Angela. He grabbed drinks off the tray and helped her hand them out.

Emmie craved a warm coffee to soothe the chill growing inside her, but she needed something strong now to soothe her mind. Maybe the sparkling green drink stuff with lime slices pushed into the ice would do the trick. It looked delicious, and she accepted a glass graciously. "I'm guessing Mojito."

Angela gestured with her head toward Flavio. "A little something he taught me how to make."

"It's called a caipirinha," Flavio answered. "A taste of my Brazilian heritage."

Emmie took a sip and the sweet taste did seem to help calm her nerves. It was like a Mojito or a Margarita, but somehow better.

Flavio watched her with curiosity. "Do you like it?"

She nodded and licked her lips. "Can you teach me how to make these?"

He nodded politely. "Of course."

Angela's parents came out from the house a moment later wearing clean clothes and took seats next to Red and Sherry. Angela sat between Emmie and Flavio and held out her glass toward each of them. "What did I miss?"

Sherry leaned forward before Emmie could answer. "Just telling your friend about the moonshiners in the area long ago. Still haven't found that stash of gold yet in all that mess over there."

"And we won't," Red finished.

Angela seemed content with her answer and leaned back in her chair.

It only took Emmie a few minutes to start feeling a little buzzed from her drink, although she hadn't even finished half of it. It had been weeks since she'd had a strong drink and the sweet taste lifted her mood.

The conversation turned to Sherry, who had started talking about her job and the difficulties of dealing with several students with behavioral and academic issues at the high school, wishing that she could just hypnotize them to get them to do what she wanted them to.

"She can do that for real, you know," Red said to Emmie. "Sherry's a trained hypnotherapist. She's been trying it out on me for years to get me to take out the trash."

They laughed but Sherry shook her head. "No, no, it's not like that. It's just something I use to help people get a better grasp on their problems. Help with remembering things and stopping bad habits. It's very useful in psychotherapy." She glanced around at each of them. "I can do it now. Anyone want to volunteer?"

Marty shook his head. "Kelsey and I better sit this one out. Flavio will go through all our alcohol if we leave him in charge of the drinks, and I know when to take out the trash."

"I don't blame you," Red said. "I'm not sure I want my wife inside my head, either."

Sherry jabbed him with her elbow. "I've seen what's inside your head, and I'm still married to you."

Red swallowed. "I better stop there."

"Good call." Sherry looked at Angela, Flavio, and Emmie in turn. "Anyone?"

Emmie kept her hands firmly against her chair, but waiting for one of them to volunteer was a torturous pause that lasted a few awkward seconds. Sherry's expression saddened, although Emmie was not about to make herself vulnerable in front of her new friends.

Finally, Flavio lifted his hand. "I'll do it."

Emmie watched him for a moment. *So thoughtful to not leave Sherry hanging.*

Sherry's face brightened. "Wonderful!" She moved to the

edge of her chair and extended her hand palm down toward Flavio. "Watch my fingertips."

He did and followed Sherry's instructions by focusing on her fingers with the hint of a grin as if humoring her.

She put her hand on his shoulder and spoke in a soothing, soft voice. "Relax and let go." As she induced him to close his eyes, the self-conscious grin on his face melted away. He wavered within a minute as the words seemed to take effect.

"Relax," Sherry repeated over and over. "Concentrate on the smell of the trees and the wind against your skin." The soothing imagery seemed to lull him into a peaceful stillness.

At the same time, the surge of anxiety Emmie had felt earlier now didn't seem so important. Sherry spoke so softly, so convincingly, that it made perfect sense that she also should... relax.

Angela also stood and crept up beside him, taking the soiled towel from the chair that he had discarded earlier and placing it under his nose. "I brought you something, Flavio. This sweet bouquet. Smell it."

Kelsey and Red cringed, each letting out a delighted laugh. Sherry smirked and shook her head. "That's just cruel."

But Angela did it anyway, pressing the towel under his nose. "Do you smell the roses, Flavio?"

He sniffed with a bright smile and nodded. "Yes."

"Take a good whiff."

He sniffed again, then started to cough before he shook his head and opened his eyes. Looking around at each of them with a confused look on his face, he turned back to Angela. "I'm disappointed, Angela. I expected you to mess with me, but... my towel?"

"I couldn't resist."

He tossed away the towel. "I think I was even starting to feel something."

Sherry seemed annoyed at the interruption in her process. "We can try again later, maybe with someone else?"

The laughter and conversation faded around Emmie.

Teetering in her chair as if she hovered at the edge of sleep, she set her drink aside and stood, feeling more relaxed than she had in a long time. A soft voice called to her from somewhere in the distance, a young girl's voice. She turned and walked toward the sound. It was a distant laughter, like an echo of a child playing a game, a curious voice that seemed to tug at her heartstrings. The laugh veiled something deeper, an emotional pain that was impossible to ignore.

With each step toward it, the sounds of the ocean and her new friends back at the gathering became a little more distant. It all seemed so irrelevant, but so important that she follow the laughter.

Emmie...

Someone said her name, although she couldn't tell from which direction. The voice came faintly as though a wall stood between them.

Emmie...

Someone clutched her arm, then her shoulder. Emmie wrestled away the invisible entity, but another grabbed her other side and held on.

Emmie, wake up...

The sounds of the ocean grew louder and her eyes snapped open. The light and salty air and reality crashed in as she struggled within the grasp of Angela on her left and Sherry on her right.

"Did I get to you?" Sherry asked.

Angela laughed nervously. "Looks like you did. Em, are you okay?"

Emmie nodded. "Yes."

Angela turned back toward the others. "She got hypnotized, all right."

"Oh, poor girl," Kelsey said sympathetically. "Bring her back over."

But Emmie stood still as her senses returned to her. Marty was laughing, but not in a mean way. Still, she had made a fool of herself in front of Flavio. How could she simply return to her seat now as if nothing had happened?

"I'm so sorry," Sherry said. "This does happen once in a while, where a bystander is affected."

"No harm done," Emmie said. But before turning around to face the others, she stared ahead toward the place where she had heard the laughter. A young girl of about eleven years old stood in dirty clothes at the edge of the trees blocking the view of the lighthouse.

Emmie shuddered. She blinked, and the girl was gone.

❧ 4 ❧

Everyone was watching Emmie now. They weren't making it obvious, but she could tell by the way they held her gaze just a little too long. If there were a hole nearby, she would crawl into it.

Dropping back into her seat within the circle of chairs, she cringed internally and put on a brave face. "Sorry, everyone."

"It's my fault," Sherry said.

Marty aimed a joke at Sherry. "Be more careful of where you aim that power of yours."

Emmie played along, nudging her drink away from her. "Probably just a little too much alcohol."

Flavio leaned toward her with a grin and touched her arm. "Caipirinhas will do that to you."

Emmie nodded and accepted his warm gesture. But she desperately wanted to grab her drink and down the whole thing in that moment just to calm her nerves. The temptation to do just that grew until Flavio touched her a second time and gestured toward the ocean. "Let's go for a walk. Get some fresh air."

Angela looked at Emmie and tilted her head to the side with a cheeky smile as if to say, 'You're crazy if you turn him down.'

"Sure." Emmie stood, and Flavio held out his hand for support. She accepted his help, though she didn't need it, feeling the strength and warmth of his skin against her fingers.

They walked toward the cliff but avoided glancing toward the lighthouse or back toward the others. Still, she could feel them staring at her.

The cold breeze chilled her face, and the sound of seagulls came from somewhere near the shore. There was no hint of the girl's laughter in the air anymore, thank God. But Emmie's chance to make a good first impression on Flavio and the others had slipped away.

At least, Flavio seemed to steer her toward the cliff, not the lighthouse. She did relax and her heart slowed as she took in all the beauty around her. They moved out across a rocky section and stopped several yards before reaching the edge. It wasn't a straight drop to the shoreline. The cliff sloped down gently at that location, but a little further along, back toward the lighthouse, there was nothing to stop someone from plunging over the side.

Flavio stopped and met her gaze. "Is that better?"

"Definitely." She kept her back to the lighthouse as he inched closer and studied her face. "Your hands are trembling."

Emmie glanced down at her hands. They *were* shaking like an old woman's, but the more she tried to steady them, the more they shook. Giving up, she slipped them into her pockets. "Just... cold."

He looked over her shoulder and gestured toward the lighthouse. "We can keep walking..."

"Here is fine."

"You must be curious about the lighthouse and the Davidson murders."

Emmie paused a moment to consider how to answer. Talking about it might fuel her fears, but she didn't want to end the conversation either. "Did they ever catch who killed them?"

Flavio shook his head. "The case is unsolved. They have a theory but—"

"So the murdered family, they never found justice?"

"I'm afraid not, in this case. It's rare that—"

"A child too?"

Flavio got a solemn look. "Lily. Maybe no one would have ever known about the child's neglect if it hadn't happened. And when everyone found out what had been happening to her, it was too late. The poor girl—"

"Sorry to interrupt," Angela said apologetically, coming up beside Emmie with a drink in one hand and looking at each of them.

Flavio turned toward Angela and stepped back. "You're not interrupting."

Angela circled around and stared into Emmie's face, gently touching her chin and turning her face to the side. "Your face is pale, like you've seen a ghost!"

"Is it?" Emmie covered her face where Angela had touched.

"Probably just the cold air." Flavio rubbed her shoulder. "She'll survive."

Angela's eyes narrowed at him. "And you're helping her to warm up?"

Flavio smirked. "She's a bit shaken."

"I think I put too much rum in those drinks," Angela said. "I'm a terrible bartender."

Emmie shook her head. "I probably just drank them too fast."

Flavio shook his head. "No, this place has a heavy vibe." He glanced around until stopping at Angela.

"Since when do you believe in vibes?" Angela asked. "It was all a long time ago."

"True." Flavio nodded once as if the conversation had ended.

Emmie glanced back toward the fire pit. The others had resumed their conversation, seemingly not paying any attention to her anymore.

"You *are* shaken." Angela met her gaze. "Maybe we'll start a small fire on the side to warm you up."

Emmie nodded, and had no intention of leaving Flavio's side, but Angela put her arm over Emmie's shoulder and led her away.

"We'll just take it easy for the rest of the night," Angela said. "I'll even let you sleep in tomorrow morning. I promised you rest and relaxation on our vacation and I intend to keep my word."

The three of them returned to the fire pit where Red and Sherry were inching toward the driveway. The conversation had shifted back to the architectural treasures they'd salvaged that day. Red seemed particularly pleased at their progress and predicted the lighthouse would be ready for demo ahead of schedule.

But as he backed away, he turned toward them. "We'll be here tomorrow to pick out more of the salvage. Still a lot to do, but it's better to stay away from it for now. We cleared out most of the debris but it's still falling apart in every direction." He stared at her. "I wouldn't go in there if I were you or even around it."

5

I *wouldn't go in there if I were you.*

Emmie slipped into bed as Red's words echoed in her mind.

Done.

I won't go in there or even look *at the damn place.*

Her heart sank as she considered her options. How would Angela feel if she asked to leave early?

She'd feel awful.

I can't leave now. Not going to happen.

The spirits were always around, weren't they? There was just no getting away from them, no matter how far she ran. And the spirits were always trying to get to her, to talk, to tell her something, and now, even at the edge of civilization they had found her. Even there, among the trees and the ocean and the serenity.

The hypnosis hadn't affected her any more than anyone else. It hadn't manifested the spirits or attracted their attention, but it had lowered her defenses so that her mind had drifted, opening herself to notice them again.

The hypnosis had caught her off guard.

Still, I should have known. I should have walked away as soon as they started messing with that stuff.

But how could she have known that a child's spirit would have found her in that one moment? The girl's presence hovered at the edge of Emmie's mind. She pressed her eyes together—painfully together—as if to squeeze it out of her mind by force.

The girl had seen her even from that distance and now it would try to grab her attention.

She shuddered, then turned on her side, pulling the covers up to her chin.

And they had all noticed her reaction. Her fear. The sinking feeling in her chest swelled over her body. She would get on a bus and ride out of there that very moment, if she could.

Yes, her "gift" of seeing the spirits of dead children had faded after moving from Minnesota to California, but now it had come back with a vengeance. Training herself to tune them out by hyper focusing on the living had helped, but now this one had slipped through after inadvertently lowering her defenses during the hypnosis session. The vulnerability of that moment had shifted her thoughts, opening her awareness to *them* like removing polarized glasses.

She could see clearly again, and dread swept through her.

So what made this spirit so much stronger than the rest? The location? The time of year? The horrific tragedy that someone had cut the girl down at such a young age? They were all tragic, all painful to see, all more than she could handle.

She could only pray that the spirit didn't follow her back to the house. They rarely followed her, but sometimes...

No, she had only seen it from a distance. Most of the time they stayed where they had died, for whatever reason, refusing to wander from where the trauma had occurred. Of course, the girl would stay away. And Emmie would also stay away.

"I won't go to your lighthouse, Red," she whispered into the sheets. "No chance of that. I'll listen. I won't go into that damn place, not for anything."

They couldn't travel very far anyway. At least, that was her theory. They were lost and fear kept them from straying too far from the trauma. So the girl was lost and would remain that way until she finally accepted what had happened. She couldn't help the spirits anyway. How could anyone help them? They had died, so what was there to do? But still they pleaded as if expecting her to rescue them somehow. But the pain in their eyes always pierced her heart. Too much pain for anyone to take in. No, there was nothing she could do that would free them from their perpetual agony.

Pushing aside all thoughts of the girl, she forced herself to clear her mind of everything as she had trained herself to do long ago.

But the wind outside pushed against the window and creaked as the ocean breeze swept over the house. The sound almost soothed her like a gentle whisper.

With her eyes closed and the darkness gently rocking her to sleep, something tapped at the window. Three quick taps, like a bird's beak pecking at the glass to test its limits.

"You can't come in," she mumbled.

Her mind cleared again as the silence lulled her again to the edge of sleep.

Three more taps. Then something scraping against the glass followed the clicks as if the bird were now using its claws to pry away the window's frame.

Whatever it was, it wasn't giving up.

You know damn well it's not a bird.

She tensed. *It is a bird.*

Cracking her eyes open, she stared at the door to her room. The window was at the bottom of her vision near her feet and she could turn to face whatever it was, but she resisted. No blinds covered the window. Her room was on the second story, so why close them? But now it was all too easy to just turn her head and look at...

Emmie yanked the blankets up over her mouth and up to her ears. Breathing through her nose, her hot breath puffed out under the blanket. The frustration and fear surged. She was warm and cozy and sleep was within reach... if only she could grab it.

Three more taps.

There was no sense in pretending. It wasn't a bird. It was never just the wind or a shadow or her imagination. Always the thing she feared. They never left her alone, and she was a fool to think that a vacation would somehow change all that.

"What do you want from me?" she asked the silent, still air, as if she might have a conversation through the glass. "I can't help you. I can't ever help any of you."

Clenching the edge of the blankets, she held back a scream. She had already made a fool of herself. They had all seen that something was weird about her, that something was off. Waking up Angela's family, even if she justified it as a nightmare, wouldn't help to dispel those first impressions.

Better that I cut and run before it gets worse. I won't be able to sleep anyway.

She doubted that Angela would invite her next summer—not that it mattered anymore. It was more important that she get herself out of that situation before things got worse. She could call an Uber, leave a note that she wasn't feeling well and be done with it without any of the drama. Fly by night. Yes, better that I—

Three more taps.

Emmie winced. If she intended to get out of there, she would need to get up and get ready and the girl's face would be there.

From the corner of her eye, a dark form appeared beyond the glass. A chill swept through Emmie, the same icy chill she'd experienced so many times before.

If I meet her eyes again, I'll see her trauma and the pain.

Emmie pressed her eyes shut again like a scared child. "Go away," she whispered. "Please go away."

With her pulse thumping in her ears, each breath moved shallow and fast, and she squeezed her eyes together until it ached. There was no light as she tensed while waiting for the taps to again rattle her nerves.

I'll go to Angela's room.

She shook her head. How would that look? She was twenty-one.

But how would she manage her life with such a "gift"? How would she ever make friends again if she didn't learn to cope with it? The thought terrified her almost as much as seeing the spirits. And how could she expect anyone to understand what she went through when even she didn't understand it?

Tears welled up in her eyes even as the tapping sound continued over the next hour. Pushing her fingers into her ears helped a little, but the tapping faded as she surrendered to the powerlessness and drifted off to sleep.

6

Emmie put on her jacket and cautiously stepped outside. She needed to get some fresh air after the encounter with the "little bird" at her window the previous night. The anxiety had kept her from looking out any windows all morning, even as Kelsey had served her pancakes for breakfast while Angela was getting ready upstairs.

The woman had dished out the pancakes with precision and efficiency as she juggled a few other tasks in the kitchen, while telling Emmie to get outside—in no uncertain terms—and take advantage of all the opportunities during her stay. Kelsey had even gestured to the windows a few times, but Emmie had kept her eyes on the woman's unwavering intensity. Better to keep her focus on the living when a spirit manifested. Day or night, it didn't matter. They seemed to appear at all hours of the day, whether she was ready for them or not. Her heightened state of anxiety was something she had learned to live with long ago, and now the presence of the girl's spirit had ruined any chance of truly letting her guard down to enjoy the moment.

She scanned the yard and her peripheral vision for any "figures." Nothing. Perhaps the girl's spirit had returned to ground zero, the location of her trauma. Even so, Emmie couldn't entirely relax. But in her experience, they *always* came back, didn't they?

She dreaded the thought of staying in that bedroom another night. But what excuse might she use to leave?

I don't feel well. Angela would offer to take her to the doctor.

A family emergency came up. Angela knew she didn't have any family nearby, and also knew she wasn't close to them.

Only a grand excuse could get her out of there without making a scene or hurting feelings.

I saw a ghost and I want to get the hell out of here.

Emmie groaned. Her heart sank at the realization she was stuck in that place for the duration of her spring break. She would need to get through it one way or another. She could do it, reluctantly, just as she had all her life. And her friendship with Angela meant too much to risk offending her with an early retreat.

The air was fresh and cold as the fog had cleared away, revealing a more vibrant environment of stone and grass and trees that she hadn't fully taken in the day before. The sun cast long shadows over the yard and the morning dew seemed to twinkle over every surface. She had put on her jacket, remembering how cold it could get in the morning near the ocean with the wind whipping in unchallenged, but despite the chilly air brushing her hair and face, it was refreshing to reconnect with nature.

With a little apprehension, she glanced back and spotted her bedroom window. There was nothing to indicate anything had physically caused the noises up there the previous night. No branches nearby, and only a narrow windowsill. Of course, it hadn't been a bird and there was no chance an animal might have climbed up there.

As she turned back toward the ocean, tree branches creaked ahead and birds chirped around her. The sounds of the wildlife waking up almost drowned out a familiar knocking sound that came from somewhere beneath the pile of wood in the fire pit. Three knocks, then silence.

The cold air seemed to freeze her bones. She stared at the source of the sounds, a section of the scrap wood that had collapsed around a window frame. There was an opening within the pile, filled with a thick darkness, and wide enough for some-one, someone small—a child—to climb through. As she stared, one of the boards at the top of the pile broke free and tumbled down, coming to a stop at the bottom of the opening.

The wind or the damp surface must have loosened it.

Then another piece dropped, landing inches from the first. Something shifted in the pile, almost imperceptibly pushing through the scraps.

Emmie swallowed and inched back.

An animal? It had made its home in the pile while they slept. And in a moment, the thing would jump out of there and back into the forest where it had come from.

But instead of an animal, a hand emerged. Thin pale fingers curled around the edges of the window's frame and strained as a head of long brown hair poked out, her face gaunt and soiled as if she'd slept in the woods for days. Her arms emerged as she pulled herself forward and plucked the piece of wood that had fallen near the opening.

Lily.

Mercifully, the girl didn't look up, and Emmie couldn't run in that moment if she'd tried. Grabbing the second loose piece, the girl wedged it against the wall of the opening, propping up the crooked frame that defined the hole.

The wood pile shook for a few seconds, and several more pieces broke loose. The girl gathered each piece from the small avalanche and stacked them within the opening as if to seal herself inside.

Was Lily trying to bury herself? Or build a fort?

But before the last piece had sealed her in, the top of the girl's head poked out again. The gnarled curls in her disheveled hair brushed against the edge of the frame as her pale face turned sharply toward Emmie. Wide brown eyes met Emmie's gaze.

"... run?" Angela's voice came from behind her.

Emmie shuddered and spun around. Her friend had dressed in a cream tank top and yoga pants and was pulling back her long, beautiful hair into a ponytail over and over as if she couldn't seem to get it exactly the way she liked. A headband and wristbands both proudly displayed the Nike corporate logo. "What?"

Angela looked at her curiously while finally tying back her hair. "Feel like a run? Or a walk or a hike? There are plenty of trails nearby, or we could take a hike down by the shore."

Emmie cupped her hands together to keep them from trembling. "Yes. Can we go now?"

Angela glanced over toward the wood pile. "Something hiding in there?"

"Just a squirrel, I think." Following Angela's gaze, the opening and the girl were both gone with no sign they had ever been there.

Angela turned back to Emmie and looked her over for a moment. "Are you feeling okay?"

Here was a chance to build a case to leave early, but the sincerity in Angela's eyes reminded Emmie that she wasn't alone. Angela truly cared and had opened her heart and family by inviting Emmie along. She couldn't just feign a sickness and leave because a spirit had found her. They would find her no matter how far she ran. She would just have to deal with the nightly encounters. "Maybe just a little hung over."

Angela grinned. "You didn't have that much. Maybe I just mixed the drink wrong. I'm so sorry. We'll take a hike down near the shore. I go there all the time, and it's not that far. Just stick to the trail down to the water and you'll be fine. There's a place near the bottom that I like to go and just sit to listen to the waves. It's so peaceful there."

Peaceful. Emmie nodded. It might be as far from the spirit as she would get during her stay. "I can't wait."

Angela glanced down at Emmie's shoes. "Converses. They tend to slip on the rocks. Have anything else in your suitcase?"

Emmie followed her gaze. "They're all I brought."

Angela gestured to her own dark gray hiking shoes with a thicker construction and secured lacing system. "These are better for hiking, especially maneuvering over the rocks in the morning with all the condensation, but you shouldn't slip *too much,* as long as you're careful."

Emmie nodded. "I'll be careful."

"Cool. Let's go." Angela led the way as they circled around the wood pile.

There was no sign of the girl now, but Emmie avoided looking at the pile directly anyway. The hairs on the back of her neck bristled until they had moved several yards past it.

They went along the side of the cliff for fifty feet before turning down a sloping trail toward the beach, zigzagging between rocks and trees and foliage. Emmie grew breathless after only a few minutes, but Angela paused often to take in the view and get Emmie's opinion.

"I try to take my friends down to the beach at least once," Angela said. "Do you like it?"

Emmie nodded. "It's like standing at the edge of the world."

"It's the best place when you need a little privacy. And a great workout. I started taking walks down here with my dad when I was little and it never grows old. Flavio likes to come down here and fish sometimes. Do you like to fish?"

"Never tried it."

"Another thing Flavio could show you." Angela continued down another slope.

They stopped again after several minutes. The trail seemed to go on forever as they descended toward the ocean with the cliff and lighthouse above them and the water crashing against the rocky shoreline only a short distance below them. A gust of wind had picked up, tossing Emmie's hair as she tried to take in all the natural beauty and the sounds of the crashing waves against the jagged rocks below. The beach was relatively small, only a hundred feet wide and ten feet deep, but the sand and seashells had mixed to produce a lovely oasis of serenity as the waves stopped at the shoreline and receded in a mesmerizing cycle.

Between her heaving breaths, Emmie asked, "Do you ever go swimming here?"

"Way too cold." Angela paused. She turned back to Emmie and feigned a deep chill. "Even in the summer, the water doesn't heat up enough to really enjoy it. Unless you are one of those polar bear types of people."

"I'm not. I prefer a sauna."

"I hear you." Angela laughed. "It's better appreciated from up here."

Glancing along the side of the cliff behind them, she focused on the lighthouse. Sections of it along the side were missing where Red and Flavio had already removed any valuable architectural pieces. The neglect was visible even from that distance. Part of the tower had collapsed with most of the glass shattered and even a section of the tower itself had broken away.

Small groups of trees dotted the area along the cliff where nature had anchored itself and somehow thrived. Behind one tree, a thick, wide bush almost obscured a small hole in the side of the cliff. It looked large enough for a person to climb through, and it sat directly beneath the lighthouse, about twenty feet from the top of the cliff.

Emmie gestured at it. "Is that a cave up there?"

Angela followed her gaze. "I suppose."

"Red said that bootleggers passed through here at one time."

Angela shrugged and continued. "Who cares what happened way back when?"

7

Returning to the house after the hike, Emmie took a shower before heading back downstairs to wait for Angela to finish doing the same.

Kelsey was out in the garden again, and Emmie watched the middle-aged woman from the kitchen window while she ripped a group of weeds from the ground with her gloved hands. Moving effortlessly, Kelsey sifted through handfuls of dirt on her hands and knees, plucking out stones that she tossed into a wheelbarrow beside her. Grabbing a garden shovel, she moved along to a different section and stabbed at the earth, seemingly focused on one spot in particular. Clawing deeper, with her arm muscles bulging, she pulled out a rock the size of a football, examined it for a moment, then tossed it into the wheelbarrow with the other foliage as if it weighed no more than the others.

Emmie had never considered herself unfit, but Angela's family seemed to set the bar for an active outdoor lifestyle.

Despite the release of stress that the hike had provided, she couldn't stop herself from glancing over at the woodpile every few seconds, wondering if the girl would emerge from the "fort" she'd built earlier. And after several minutes, Emmie assured herself that the girl wouldn't return until at least later that night.

But only a moment later, she spotted Lily dancing toward the garden as if refusing to let her pale, sickly body hold her back. She came within a few feet of Kelsey, picking non-existent flowers that materialized in her hands and drawing them out of the same area that Kelsey had cleared away only moments earlier. Lily laughed as she picked them, gathering them into an oversized bouquet that she struggled to hold and cradled them as if she couldn't get enough.

Circling around the garden with her trove of roses and daisies and daffodils, Lily bent forward before tossing them all into the air in a wide arc while laughing as the wind caught them and they disappeared.

Lily's actions caught Emmie off guard. Wasn't this the same girl who had terrorized her the previous night?

The girl's arms swung over her head, and she spun beneath the flowers as they landed in the grass around her. Emmie couldn't look away. This was the same girl, but instead of the previous night's terror, now Emmie only felt curiosity and concern as her heart went out to the girl. Her traumatic death didn't diminish her life, and she didn't deserve what had happened.

A bit of shame swept through Emmie. It was easy to forget how the spirits had gotten that way, but seeing their trauma, sometimes horrific violence, on a day-to-day basis had jaded Emmie, for good reason—most of them demanded her attention if she even glanced in their direction. Somehow, most of them knew she could see them, and they rarely let her pass without a heart-wrenching plea for help.

Those were the agonizing moments of her life, when she desperately wanted to do something for them, somehow relieve their pain, but it was always hopeless. That's why she always had to look away. The only road to sanity.

But Lily stopped playing suddenly, turned and looked at Emmie. The girl's eyes widened as if Emmie had startled her. Emmie stepped backed. Could she see her through the window from that distance? Of course she could. And Lily stared with the eyes of a curious child, tilting her head to the side, then made a wide gesture for Emmie to come outside.

The fear was gone in that moment. No need to resist the girl's invitation, so Emmie walked outside and followed the girl as she headed toward the lighthouse. Passing the garden, Emmie remembered what Flavio had said about Lily the previous night. The poor girl...

Emmie tensed in preparation for Lily to reveal some horrific scene. All the spirits tried to tell their story, if she took a moment to listen, and none of them ended on a cheerful note.

Moving to within several feet of Lily, Emmie got a full view of her. The bony frame, the unkempt hair, the emaciated face. She was just a young girl, and it was clear she'd died horribly. It pained Emmie's heart even to glimpse the tragedy for a moment.

"I know something horrible happened to you," Emmie said to Lily, then glanced back toward the house. Kelsey was still busy in the garden and hadn't seemed to notice that Emmie had walked off.

Following Lily through a group of trees that separated the property, Emmie passed a neglected utility shed before circling around the lighthouse. No cars in the driveway, so Red and Flavio hadn't started work on the lighthouse for the day yet. If they arrived while she was exploring the area, it would be an awkward moment. But she couldn't back out now. She would only see what Lily was trying to show her and then leave.

They walked toward the cliff, not far from where she and Angela had hiked earlier and stepped down a sloping landscape of rocks and brush and earth. But this wasn't the same worn path she had taken earlier. This one was more difficult to navigate, forcing her to climb up a steep sloping rock before arriving at the cave she had seen from the shoreline.

As soon as Emmie had caught up, Lily stepped inside the cave hesitantly as if she feared something inside.

"Is this where you died?" Emmie asked.

Lily didn't answer.

Several feet inside the rocky hole, a wooden door covered an entrance straight ahead. Lily moved through it effortlessly, leaving Emmie to work at the latch for a few frustrating seconds before it snapped open and she stepped inside.

The room was about the size of a small bedroom and the cool air mixed with a musty smell. Nobody had gone inside that room for a long time judging by the spiderwebs and dust that covered the floor and an assortment of antique oil lanterns and rusted metal bars that were piled against one wall. An old wooden ladder sat against the wall along the far side, rising to the ceiling.

A small bed sat against one wall. The bed's frame was antique, judging by the ornate black metal bars along the head and foot of the bed, but the twin sized mattress and a quilted blanket couldn't have been over twenty years old.

Lily moved over near the bed and stood beside it but not on it, and she stared at a wooden box in the corner of the room.

Emmie followed her eyes. "Is that what you want me to see?"

Lily nodded. Emmie knelt in front of it and opened it. A small cache of trinkets like necklaces and heart-shaped pendants and even a tiny rose the size of a quarter encased in a clear resin case with the words 'Thinking of you' etched along the front. Things someone might present to a romantic partner.

Red had mentioned something about bootleggers at that location, but the bed and the box and the trinkets couldn't have been around that long. Maybe Lily's family had used it for something. Or Lily herself.

Emmie dug through the box and discovered several notes at the bottom. She read a few of them—typed notes signed with someone's initials. PT. They were addressed to someone named Skye.

Turning back to ask Lily about them, Emmie held back her question. The girl had disappeared. Not that Lily would have answered any questions anyway.

Emmie glanced through the notes again. The murdered woman had a lover and met him there, right below her house?

The ones on the bottom were older and full of cute language that a man might express to a lover.

"... Your eyes reflect our future, filled with love, laughter, and unwavering support for our dreams."

"... I'm grateful for every moment with you as we've explored hidden trails and unrestrained emotions."

"... I find heaven in your embrace, like nothing I've ever experienced. Such a sense of belonging and warmth that touches my soul and erases the worries of the world."

But the notes weren't all about love. The ones near the top held a different tone, pointing toward anger.

"I used to believe in your love, but now I'm questioning everything."

"So now I'm left picking up the pieces of our relationship, trying to make sense of what you've told me."

"I can't help but wonder if all the laughter we shared was just a show. Tell me the truth."

The notes were significant in some way, although she couldn't exactly make the connection. Did an affair spark someone's rage and lead to the family's murder? It *was* the perfect location to hide secrets of all kinds: bootlegging, forbidden romance... murder.

The still, silent room echoed the sounds of the ocean waves through the open door. She slipped the notes and the trinkets into the pockets of her cargo pants and buttoned them shut before staring up at the ladder. It led toward a small metal door against the ceiling.

It had to lead to somewhere in the lighthouse. The ladder's wood was thick and sturdy—no wonder it had survived for so long—and it wasn't until she had started climbing it that she connected the metal rusted bars along the wall to an old metal ladder that must've existed in the same spot at one time. Something the bootleggers had used?

She climbed up the ladder and pushed against the small door

at the ceiling. It was stuck, but it shifted upwards after a forceful thrust, opening with a loud screech. It was thick, but not too heavy, and she pushed it off to the side as she climbed up and into the bottom floor of the lighthouse.

Around her sat a few architectural remnants that Red and Flavio must have disassembled but not yet removed. There were groupings of decorative crown moldings, transom windows with decorative glasswork, and small piles of ornamental brackets made of wood, metal, and stone. But now she took in the full extension of the structure's neglect. The painted walls were peeling away, there were signs of black mold everywhere, and rust covered everything made of metal. The windows along the tower were severely damaged and wide open, letting in all the elements. It was hard to believe the ocean had destroyed so much in just nine years—it looked as if it'd sat abandoned for a century—but without constant upkeep, it had sat defenseless against the constant barrage of wind, rain, and saltwater.

Emmie eyed a doorway straight ahead that must have led into the main house connected to the lighthouse, but a winding metal corkscrew staircase stared down at her from above. It led up toward the tower and seemed to beckon her. A landing sat halfway up near broken windows on the second story, and beyond that sunlight streamed down through an open door that could only have been the entrance to the tower.

Moving up the stairs while gripping the metal railings, she remembered Red's warning to avoid the lighthouse. Still, it might be her only chance to explore it.

At the second floor landing a minute later, she stood in a small room with broken windows and more water damage. Someone had renovated it all at one time, judging by the updated flooring and painted walls and light fixtures, but now it lay stripped away and rotting. The wind pushed through the broken glass unobstructed and brushed through Emmie's hair as she glanced around the area.

A pile of framed photos sat on the floor in the corner, and

one showed Lily's family. The girl had the same brown hair, short and healthy. She stood happily beside her parents. Lily's mother was very beautiful, with dark hair and green eyes, looking as if she'd walked out of the movies to pretend she was a housewife. Her father was shorter than her mother, and stocky, but there was a confidence in his expression, a boldness in his eyes. Women liked that type, even beautiful women. Emmie stared into Lily's eyes—the girl's playful look had the same spark of life she had shown earlier in the garden.

Nothing out of place in those photos, but family portraits rarely displayed the truth beneath the smiles.

"What happened?" Emmie asked the beaming faces in the Davidson family portrait.

The sound of a truck passed through the air. Someone had parked outside.

"Oh, shit."

Red and Flavio, no doubt. Emmie's heart raced faster. She hurried to slip the photo into her pocket along with the notes. Maybe she could use the photo later to connect with Lily's spirit.

Hurrying to start down the stairs again, the metal railings squeaked and clanked as she descended. Part of it started to shift as her weight caused it to swing from side to side. Clearly the thing wasn't stable. But she didn't have time for stealth. She hurried with her footsteps echoing around her.

Before she reached the bottom, Flavio opened the door on the first floor, and almost at the same time, something metallic cracked loose with a loud pop. She met his startled stare, his eyes wide, and his gaping mouth.

"What...?" Flavio said. "Don't move!"

Red came up behind him, spotted her, then cursed so loud that it hurt her ears.

Flavio moved in along the side of the drifting staircase below her with his arms up. "Stay near the center of the stairs. Don't step on the outside edge."

"I'm sorry." Emmie did as he said, moving slowly down step

by step, shifting her weight with as much care as she could manage.

When she reached the bottom, her heart was pounding in her ears, not just from having avoided catastrophe but also from the embarrassment of getting caught inside the lighthouse.

"What are you doing here?" Flavio didn't waste time to scold her, his voice a mix of irritation and relief.

Emmie ran her fingers over the buttons on her cargo pants to make sure that nothing had fallen out. "I came looking for you."

His expression didn't change, but it was better to face the embarrassment of a cute guy thinking she liked him than anything to do with the truth.

He held her arm for a moment, then sighed. "Are you okay?"

"Yes, thank you. You got here just in time."

"Damn right we did," Red shouted. "This place is dangerous. We're in the last phase of tearing this thing down, and you shouldn't go snooping around here by yourself. I warned you last night, and I'll say it again. Don't come in here."

Emmie opened her mouth to apologize again, but Red's face was growing more flush. Meeting his eyes for only a moment, his anger was palpable.

Why so much anger? Did he know what she was really doing there?

She hurried away without saying another word.

8

Just after lunch, Angela's family received word that an ambulance had taken Kelsey's father to the hospital after a fall at home.

"Nothing too serious," Kelsey assured Emmie while pointing out the leftover food in the fridge and house keys on a hook near the door. "But we should leave now."

"Hospitals are *so* boring." Angela walked in with her backpack and put her arm over Emmie's shoulders. "I haven't seen Grandpa in months, and he sounded a bit down on the phone, so I hope you're okay on your own for half a day?" She pulled her car keys out of her purse and handed them to Emmie. "Explore the town. Grab a coffee and relax or whatever. There's plenty to do."

Emmie clutched the set of keys and contemplated the fact that she would be alone... with Lily. "Hope your grandfather's doing all right."

Kelsey smiled. "He'll be fine."

Only seconds later, Angela and Kelsey were gone and the door shut behind them.

The silence of the house was unsettling. There was plenty she could do to keep her mind off what she had found earlier that morning, but she hadn't stopped thinking about it. It wasn't something she could ask Angela or her family about—the murders had traumatized them too much. Lily hadn't been just a neighbor, but Angela's friend, and Marty had discovered the murders.

Earlier that morning, just after she'd awakened, she'd scoured the Internet for any information about what had happened at the lighthouse, but all she could find was a few brief paragraphs confirming what the others had already said, that a burglar or burglars had murdered a local family nine years earlier.

She hadn't gone to a local library in years, but the local newspapers often wrote articles detailing information that never appeared on the Internet, especially about an old case in a small town. The library was in town, and if she was going to investigate anything, she had to act quickly. Without hesitation, she squeezed the set of keys in her hand, grabbed her jacket from a hook beside the door and headed out.

Arriving at the library twenty minutes later, Emmie entered the small, brightly lit building with a single overwhelming question nagging her mind. *What really happened?*

A gray-haired woman with glasses hanging from cords over her chest stood behind the circulation desk and offered her help with a pleasant smile.

"Where can I find old local newspaper articles?" Emmie asked. "From around nine years ago?"

"Do you mean the actual published articles?" The librarian's face lit up. "I don't get those kinds of requests much anymore from someone your age. Follow me."

The woman led Emmie to a long table with three large boxy gray devices that vaguely resembled computers along one wall at the back of the library.

They weren't anything like she had ever seen before.

The librarian seemed to wait for Emmie's reaction before continuing. "These aren't computers. Microfilm readers."

Emmie stared curiously at the old machines. "I've heard of those."

The librarian laughed softly. "We still use them from time to time. My predecessor believed that photographing the articles was a better way to preserve the town's posterity. After she retired eight years ago, we started relying more on the Internet, but you'll only find what you're looking for on the older devices, I'm afraid. She motioned to a small metal filing cabinet. The films are in this drawer, classified by time."

"I think I can get it."

Still, the librarian stepped Emmie through a quick tour of the machine's antiquated interface. Only a couple of minutes later, Emmie was alone and focused.

Finding newspaper articles related to the Davidson family murders was a matter of looking for the films under the date for the murders her search online had already yielded. She quickly found that the photographed articles from the time were much richer in detail than the Internet, as she'd hoped.

The police had discovered the couple, Paul and Skye Davidson, shot dead in their living room on the ground floor of Shine House four days after their death. The absence of their daughter, Lily, from school had alerted the authorities. They discovered the eleven-year-old girl in a separate shed, where she'd been kept captive and had eventually died of dehydration. The sheriff's office, led by Martin Allen, concluded that a home invasion had gone wrong, noting a series of similar burglaries nearby although no violence had occurred in the other cases.

One of the missing items was a gun registered in Paul Davidson's name. The sheriff concluded the burglars must've entered the lighthouse thinking it empty but were met with armed resistance and then later stole Davidson's gun.

There were more updates of the days that followed. The details of Lily's tragedy struck Emmie particularly hard. It was almost difficult to breathe as she read through all that it happened to the young girl. They had discovered her body in the shed, which had puzzled the police at first. The investigators had assumed the burglars might have imprisoned her there to spare her the violence in the house, or unable to kill a child as they fled. She'd died of natural causes because, with their parents dead, no one had thought to look for until her absence from school had drawn the attention of the teachers.

However, forensic investigators couldn't find any trace of intruders in the shed. The footprints and fingerprints belonged to the police, made when the girl was found. And it was unlikely that burglars could have covered their traces on the soft ground around the shed.

Then a testimony had shattered the community: a witness had come forward, stating the family had abused Lily for years. The authorities had allowed the witness, as a minor, to remain anonymous, but provided details of Lily's ordeal, which included punishments of being locked in the shed for days at a time. More details about Lily's parents had come to light based on the witness testimony, enraging the community.

Alone and forgotten in the shed, Lily had succumbed to thirst.

The poor girl...

Emmie's eyes watered as she remembered the little girl laughing and throwing flowers in the air near the garden. The tragedy hadn't destroyed her happiness, even after years of abuse and neglect.

But there hadn't been any signs of abuse on the girl, nothing physical anyway. Maybe she had only been locked up, not beaten. Was it possible to find out such a thing?

"Are you finding what you're looking for?" the librarian asked.

Emmie shuddered at the woman's voice and spun around to face her. How long had she been standing there? "Yes, thank you. I think so."

By the librarian's pursed lips and frown, it was clear the woman had been reading over Emmie's shoulder and that she didn't approve. There was no sign of the woman's earlier cheerfulness as Emmie switched off the machine and put the micro-films back in their drawer.

Thanking the librarian with a wave, Emmie left in a hurry.

Outside, the cool air dried her eyes as she took deep breaths to help clear away the emotional pain of Lily's story. No wonder Flavio had stopped talking suddenly when Angela approached them. He was only thinking of Marty's family and the trauma they must have endured after their neighbor was murdered. Angela was the same age as Lily at the time of the murder, so they must have not only been neighbors but close friends. That little girl had sat for days, probably begging for help, not far from their house.

It was unthinkable.

Marty knew all about the case, but Emmie could never ask him anything. It was obviously a taboo topic, and no wonder. However, Flavio had access to the police files on the case, and he *had* seemed willing to discuss it away from Angela and her parents. *Maybe...*

Emmie pulled out her phone, found the contact for Flavio she'd saved the night before, and texted him.

9

Emmie met Flavio at a small, quaint coffee shop in town. There were plenty of tables available inside, but she picked one with more privacy outside, away from the customers entering and leaving.

Flavio paid for her drink, and they sat across from each other with the sun gently warming her face. His police uniform was a stark contrast to the casual outfit he'd worn at Angela's house, but it suited him, in a way. He seemed more competent without intimidating her.

Sipping his coffee, he looked at her curiously. "You said you wanted to ask me a question?"

"Yes." Emmie tensed at the thought of the notes in her pocket. "Yes. It's... something I found in the lighthouse."

He frowned. "You went in there *again*?"

"Not exactly. I mean, I actually went into a sort of a cave below it, and I followed it up... into the lighthouse. The smugglers might have used it?"

"Red warned you to stay out. It's very dangerous in there. You could have gotten hurt."

"I won't go back. Promise. But I found these..."

She dug out the notes from her pocket and showed them to

him, making sure the Davidson family photos remained in her pocket. No sense in stoking his disapproval by revealing she'd also climbed up all the way to the tower. Better to keep him focused on what she'd brought him there for.

He nodded toward the notes. "What's all this?"

"These are addressed to Lily's mom, Skye." Emmie watched his reaction for a moment. "I'm sure you're familiar with the details of what happened, but I think these notes suggest a different story. They might suggest a different motive for the murders."

Flavio moved back in his chair and his eyes widened. "What do you mean?"

She gestured to the notes. "I mean, maybe it wasn't burglars after all, like Marty thought, but someone else. If you read the notes in order..."

He appeared to hesitate for a moment, probably wondering what was in it for her. But then his eyes started skimming over the words and he flipped through the notes back and forth as if following the narrative through just as she had hours earlier. His expression changed from confusion to disapproval to shock. When he was done, he titled his head to one side as his dark eyes seemed to focus on the empty space between them.

He gets it.

The official story didn't add up anymore.

Flavio touched his hand to his chin. "Lily's mom, Skye, *was* beautiful. An ex-model, if I remember right. We even thought so as kids, when she came to get Lily in school. But this does sound like an affair."

"One of the reasons for murder. A jealous lover?"

Flavio flipped through the notes again, stopping at one. He scanned it quickly before reading the words out loud. *"We are lying to so many people, but we swore to tell the truth to each other. You broke your promise. You led me on."* He nodded slowly. "Looks like the lover wanted Lily's mom, and she decided to stay with her husband. It appears he blamed her for that."

The wheels were turning behind his eyes, spinning as fast as her own mind as they connected the dots.

"The story of the burglary was what the police came up with at the time," Emmie said. "But they possibly couldn't think of any personal reasons for the Davidsons to be killed. No evidence pointing to anything else." Emmie fanned out the notes again and pointed to the initials at the bottom of all the notes. "PT. Was there anyone the family might've known with those initials?"

Flavio scratched his chin. "As far as I know, no one around has those initials. I'd have to—" He broke off and shot her a look with narrowed eyes. "Why are you so interested in this case, anyway?"

Because I've met Lily.

But she couldn't say that or reveal anything about her troubling reality. Emmie tensed while choosing her response and a wave of emotion swept through her.

"Lily was just a little girl," she said finally. Genuine tears welled up in her eyes. Flavio's eyes seemed to respond to hers in the same way. He had a good heart. She knew it. "And she was your friend too, right?"

He looked away. "Yeah."

"Don't *you* want to know the truth?"

He scoffed. "Of course. But knowing who killed the Davidsons won't change what happened to Lily—the horrible way she died, trapped alone in the shed. Maybe Skye *did* have an affair and someone got revenge."

"Would that someone have abandoned Lily in the shed to die?"

For a few seconds, he only stared at her, then broke it off abruptly. "I'll do a little research and get back to you."

"When?" Emmie prodded.

Flavio held up a hand as if to calm her. "If I find anything, I'll let you know. But"—he leaned in and lowered his voice—"do *not* go into the lighthouse on your own again. We don't want another corpse, Emmie."

She nodded while meeting his stern stare. He wasn't mincing his words, but it was for her own good. "Understood."

He stood up, and she followed him.

Walking together toward his Sheriff's cruiser, he paused and turned toward her. "Also, don't tell anyone about what you found yet, especially Angela. You can't imagine what this is like for her, even after all these years." He looked around before he added, "You see, Angela is the one who found Lily."

❧ 10 ❧

Emmie couldn't help but look at Angela in a new light when her friend returned late that afternoon. No wonder she didn't talk about what had happened next door. It must have deeply traumatized her. A child finding another child dead and seeing it up close for the first time—the death and cruelty. Had Angela blamed herself for what had happened? That would be the greatest cruelty.

Seeing Angela's radiant face, Emmie longed to reach out and console her friend.

Angela seemed to pick up on Emmie's concern. "Grandpa is fine. Sorry we took so long, but he was so happy to see us." Her smile turned mischievous. "But I heard you wasted no time..."

Kelsey let out a little laugh as she passed by. "Your coffee with Flavio is making rounds on the discussion boards." She grinned and winked. "You can't hide anything in this place."

But someone can. Emmie kept the thought to herself and let the joke about Flavio pass. Let them believe what they wanted. Flirting with a cute cop was a better explanation than the truth.

Red arrived in the kitchen moments later and mercifully took the attention away from her. He was looking for Marty to join him in unloading the scrap wood from the cargo bed, but

Marty had disappeared, and Kelsey donned her workman's gloves and went out with him instead. Angela had gone to wash and change, and Emmie found herself outside, watching the pile of wood grow a little taller and wider. Her heart beat a little faster when the wood buried the spot where Lily had hidden within her "fort" that morning.

Moving in closer, she guessed that the piece on top was a thin, wide plank that appeared to have been taken from a bedroom wall, judging by the childish wallpaper still clinging to one side. Lily's?

She was still trying to digest her pain at the image of that innocence, expressed by the ballerinas and unicorns, when Sherry spoke behind her. "You went to the library, didn't you?"

Emmie turned. The question sounded more like an accusation, but it wouldn't surprise her if the librarian had discreetly checked into her background. She was from a small town herself and anything an outsider did was considered news. "Yes."

"Honey, I know I started it by telling you what happened, but now you should leave that story well alone." The sympathy in Sherry's voice was gone. "The death of that girl, Angela's little friend, is still incredibly painful. It was a horrible tragedy, and nobody has ever really gotten over it. People won't love you for asking around about that for no reason..."

Was there a hard glint in Sherry's soft blue eyes—like a warning for Emmie to stop looking into the murders—or was it her imagination?

"Are we clear?" Sherry asked with a relentless intensity.

Definitely not her imagination. "Yes."

The woman's demeanor seemed to soften as she walked away. Why was it a problem for Emmie to discreetly read about what had happened? Stirring up such a trauma wasn't good, but it was only natural that she might want to read about the murders on her own.

And had Sherry let the others know about her library visit?

Her heart sank. She certainly hoped not. She never would have intentionally hurt Angela or her parents by snooping.

A sinking sensation swept through her. Now she just felt awful.

Sherry had joined Red, and she wiped the hair out of his face while looking into his eyes as he massaged his arm muscles. Angela walked over to Emmie and looked where her friend was looking.

"Aren't they cute?" Angela gestured to them. "They look like the happiest couple, don't they? To think they almost divorced ten years ago..."

"Really? What happened?"

"Sherry almost left him, but that's just between you and me. Something I heard Mom tell Dad, that Red had been unfaithful to her. All under the bridge now though."

Emmie watched the couple. Angela was right. There truly was no sign that anything had ever come between them.

Angela shrugged. "I guess that's more of what true love looks like."

"What's Red's real name?" Emmie asked abruptly. "I assume Red is his nickname, because of his red hair."

"Yeah, you're right. Just a nickname. Charlie's his real name. Charlie Webber."

That wasn't PT—but maybe the man had another nickname? Or the initials matched his middle name?

The questions were piling up, but she had already attracted too much attention in town. There had to be a better way of checking out Red without arousing the anger of his formidable, *and so loving* wife.

It was impossible to ignore the lighthouse towering over them as Emmie and Angela hiked the trail descending toward the shoreline the next morning.

"So what did you find at the library?" Angela asked. "About Lily."

Emmie had been staring out across the water toward a group of seagulls in the distance. But now she hid her surprise and turned back to look at Angela. The sun seemed to shine directly into her face as she contemplated how to answer.

"It's okay," Angela continued calmly. "I don't blame you for wanting to know more about what happened. That's what I've been trying to figure out for half my life."

"I'm sorry I looked into it. I know it seems like I was being overly curious or nosy."

"No, nothing like that." Angela stared out toward the ocean. "But you probably know that I found Lily's body after the murders."

Emmie only nodded solemnly.

"Everyone avoids talking about it, but I'm sure that they talk when I'm not around. Nobody wants me to feel the pain over what happened, but that's impossible."

"Oh, Angela." Emmie reached out and touched her friend's shoulder. Angela didn't move away but her gaze remained distant.

"I suppose curiosity is normal. Everyone is tiptoeing around this for my benefit, telling you things in bits and pieces. They don't want to come right out and say the truth. I understand why, because they don't want to hurt my feelings, but"—now she turned to Emmie, with her eyes full of pain—"you should know the truth. I found Lily locked in the shed. And that's not the worst part..."

"Angela..."

"No, I need to talk about this. The worst part is I could have saved her."

"Oh, no. Angela—"

Angela raised a hand, asking for her silence. "It's true, and I can't stop thinking about it."

A moment of silence passed between them as Angela seemed to recompose herself. Emmie wanted to say something kind, but her friend needed a sympathetic ear in that moment.

Finally, Angela made a small gesture forward and started walking. "We should keep going."

Emmie followed by her side.

Angela continued, "I knew Lily was being abused, you see..."

The witness. From the article Emmie had read the previous day. The minor who'd come forward but had been allowed to remain anonymous. The sheriff's own daughter. As a school friend and neighbor, and Lily's own age, of course Angela would have known, or suspected, what was happening.

"She told me when I saw bruises on her, but she begged me not to tell anyone." Angela dug her fingers into her arms as she held them crossed over her chest. Her nails were short, but she left red marks as she shifted uncomfortably. "I said my dad would do something about it, but Lily was afraid of what her life would be like if social services took her away. She still loved her parents even after all that they did to her. She told me there were times when everything was okay, and they only locked her in the shed when she was really disobedient. She said they didn't beat her or anything. It seemed... less serious because of that? I knew that kids did get taken away from their parents sometimes for stuff like that and she had asked me not to tell, so I kept my word."

Angela stopped and shivered, her eyes lowered.

"So that little girl, my friend, spent days probably screaming and asking for help in that shed..." She motioned to the waves. "And you can hear what it's like here. It's loud. I didn't go near the shed back then. I had no reason to. Only when she missed school for a few days days, and then it was too late..."

The anguish on Angela's face intensified and Emmie couldn't hold back. She reached out and grabbed her friend by the hands. "Angela, you just thought you were doing the right thing. You were just a kid too."

"No, Emmie, that's no excuse. If I had told my father, Lily wouldn't have been in that shed. If I had gone out looking for her on the first day she missed school, she would have lived. She was just a little girl! She didn't have to die."

Seeing Emmie step closer, Angela moved back, shaking her head. It seemed her friend wanted no consolation. So much regret behind those pained eyes. Instead, Angela walked ahead, motioning for Emmie to give her a moment, and stopped at the edge of the shoreline with her back turned as if she had turned away from everyone she loved. Angela's confidence and happiness were gone, replaced by a fragility that Emmie had never seen before.

Why must we all be broken, even in secret?

Her heart went out to her friend, and although no words could erase Angela's grief, she instinctively stepped forward to go to her friend's side.

But a loud crash filled the air behind Emmie. She stopped suddenly, like a deer in headlights.

Red's voice screamed from above. "Look out!"

E mmie spun around, her body tensing in fear and shock as a massive metal pipe crashed down the side of the cliff toward her. The clanging object knocked an avalanche of rocks and debris as it picked up speed.

Angela screamed behind Emmie. But she was too far away to help.

The object would slam into her within seconds. Stumbling back, Emmie's Converses slipped on the damp stones until she managed to launch herself to the side, landing behind a knee-high boulder that shielded her only a moment before it bore the full brunt of the metal object. A shower of rocks, stones and dirt cascaded over her while she scrambled to shield herself even after the object had come to a rest. A delayed torrent of pain flashed through her body just after the debris had slammed into her legs, arms, and back.

"Emmie!" Angela cried out again, her footsteps crunching closer over the stones to get to her.

She rolled over onto her back as another wave of pain throbbed at the back of her head. Staring up at the sky, she spotted a group of seagulls fluttering away.

"Are you okay?" Angela asked in a panicked voice.

Emmie nursed her arm and touched the back of her head as she tried to sit up. "What was that?"

"Oh my God, Em! I don't know what happened."

Red was rushing down the trail along the edge of the cliff to get to them, and Flavio was close behind him.

Glancing around in a daze, Emmie spotted the object that had almost slammed into her. The thick metal pipe resembled something like a rusted iron water pipe about eight feet long. The thing must have weighed over a hundred pounds judging by its thickness and the way it had shattered through rocks on the way down, like an unstoppable tumbling railcar.

As her mind reeled to make sense of what had happened, Emmie staggered to her feet and brushed herself off with Angela's help. Red arrived moments later.

"Are you all right?" Red asked. "You need an ambulance?"

Emmie shook her head slowly, the throbbing pain gaining strength. "I don't think anything's broken."

"Still..." Flavio scanned her clothes. His gaze stopped on her arm. "You're bleeding."

Following his eyes to her elbow, she spotted the patch of blood and the source—a cut about two inches long, but not too deep.

Angela brushed the hair along the back of her friend's neck. "Oh, my parents will agonize over this when they come back. You almost died! We'll leave them a note, and—"

"I'll take you into town," Flavio said. "They can find us there."

Emmie shook her head with more emphasis. "I'm all right." She gave a nervous laugh. "Really. Just a little shaken."

"You'll probably have bruises in the morning." Angela looked at Red. "Is it a piece of your salvage?"

Distress swept over Red's face. "I'm sorry! I go on about safety, and then..." He scratched his head, then stared toward the top of the cliff. "I don't get it. I had that thing in a secure spot.

How could it have broken free or rolled away? Gravity alone couldn't have just moved it..."

Angela held Emmie's hand while helping her move out of the rocks and debris. "Thank God she's safe."

Flavio kicked one of the larger rocks out of her way and offered his arm for additional support. Emmie took it, though she was in no danger of falling.

Reaching the top of the cliff, Flavio released Emmie's hand after watching her for a moment with concern.

"I'll get her to the house." Angela took Emmie's arm.

Flavio nodded once then turned back toward the trail with Red beside him.

Emmie watched them descend to the shoreline, reaching the metal pipe a short time later. Looking around as if trying to figure out how the thing had fallen, Flavio eventually glanced up at Emmie. Even from that distance she could tell he was confused and even a little worried, but Angela was pulling her toward the house and out of sight.

"Red is a bit reckless with that stuff sometimes," Angela said as they paused near the garden.

"It's not his fault," Emmie said. But the accident and the hike up the trail had weakened Emmie, so she took a seat at a picnic table closer to the house.

Angela held out her hands, palms down. "Stay seated. I'll be right back."

Before Emmie could reply, Angela had rushed into the house.

Taking in deep breaths, still tasting the dirt and sand in her mouth from the accident, Emmie spotted Lily near the cliff toward the lighthouse. The girl stood in front of the path to the place where the runaway pipe had sat earlier.

The door to the front door swung open again a moment later and Angela returned with a first-aid kit, opening it with great care. "Sometimes what seems like a scratch ends up being much worse."

Emmie examined the cut near her elbow again. "It doesn't seem too bad."

Angela didn't seem to hear her. Instead, her friend went ahead with nursing the wound, covering it with a piece of gauze and bandage before settling back. "How does that feel?"

"Better," Emmie lied. "Much better."

"Does it hurt anywhere else?"

"Feels like I've been through a boxing match."

"I have to get you an icepack and some Advil or you'll swell up."

"Oh, maybe you're right." Emmie sounded more helpless than she felt, but she needed Angela to leave so she could find Lily, and Angela did, running into the house again.

As soon as Angela disappeared, Emmie spotted Lily again. The girl beckoned to Emmie as if urgently wanting to show her something. It was true that every muscle throbbed, and Emmie longed for an Advil, but Lily was waiting for her.

Emmie stood and followed her. At the edge of the cliff, Emmie looked down. Red and Fabio were gone now, along with the metal pipe. The girl continued walking, now only several feet ahead of her, until she disappeared behind some trees along the way. When Emmie reached the other side, Lily was gone.

But the pipe that Red and Flavio must have carried to the top of the cliff was there. It was far from the edge of the cliff now and turned perpendicular to it so there'd be no chance for it to roll away again.

Stepping over to the place where it had sat before toppling over the edge, Emmie spotted fresh footprints in the dirt, some of them leading off toward the cliff where someone might have dug in their feet to... push it off the cliff? Or had Red left those marks when he had placed it there? She couldn't be a hundred percent sure, but the track marks seemed to have been made by feet slipping backward while someone pushed a heavy weight.

Had someone intentionally pushed the pipe, knowing that she was directly in its path?

A brooding panic swelled in her chest, and she remembered Flavio's worried face. Was she making too much out of it? But Lily had led her there to tell her something. The girl wouldn't have called her over for no reason.

Still, if someone had intended to do her harm, either as a warning or to kill her, Red couldn't have done it. He had warned her just in time. He had saved her life.

E mmie spent the rest of the day in the house, shaken and
exhausted. Angela was right there by her side the whole
time, and they filled the day by binge-watching a favorite series
on Netflix. Their long conversations between the episodes lifted
Emmie's spirits—she even broke out laughing on a few occasions
—and it seemed to relieve some of the stress from that morning.

Still, she couldn't get what had happened out of her mind.
Someone had intentionally tried to scare or hurt her. That much
was clear. She had resolved not to speak openly about the
murders anymore. It was probably better that way, at least until
she could make sense of things.

The next morning, Kelsey invited them to go with her into
town to get some things for the bonfire and other supplies. It
couldn't wait, and Marty had already left for town that morning.

"I'll stay with Emmie." Angela spoke like a concerned sister.

"You go," Emmie said. "I could use some more rest, and
maybe I'll even go for a walk."

Angela looked into Emmie's eyes as if evaluating her condi-
tion. "I can't just leave you here alone again."

"I insist. You need to take care of all those things for the
party, and I'd feel terrible if anything got delayed over what

happened. Don't let me hold you back. Please, everything will be fine with me. Go with your mom. She needs your help too."

Angela nodded slowly, her eyes full of concern. "I suppose you *are* looking better. I'll leave my keys by the door anyway, just in case you change your mind and want to head into town for anything."

"I probably won't leave... but thank you."

"Call me if you need anything."

Only thirty minutes later, the house was empty again. Despite her bruises and aching muscles, she made her way out to the living room and stared across the ocean. The questions just kept piling up and there was only just so much she could answer on her own. She needed to talk with Flavio again.

A text message from Flavio only a few minutes later gave her the excuse to reach out to him.

Flavio: How are you holding up?

Emmie: Can you meet me somewhere alone? Discreet, not at the station.

It showed he'd read the text, but he didn't answer. His response came back several minutes later.

Flavio: I'm coming to you, but I won't park there. Meet me at the park down the road from the lighthouse in 30 minutes. Can you walk that far?

Emmie: I've got Angela's car. I'll be there.

She arrived at the small, isolated park minutes later and when Flavio arrived in his uniform, holding up a folder as he stepped from the deputy sheriff's squad car, a rush of relief passed through her. At least she wasn't alone in thinking that the killer was still at large.

He said nothing as he approached her, only taking a seat next to her at a picnic table and nodded toward the file. "I said I would look, and I did. I can't swear to anything, but the things I've seen..." He opened the file but kept his hand over it while meeting her eyes. "It's—it's pretty disturbing, Emmie. For someone who hasn't seen stuff like this."

"I have," she said simply.

He threw her a sharp look and paused as if waiting for an explanation.

His intense interest alarmed her, but it was the right moment to share a little clarity about her past. She had to gain his trust, make him understand she was no stranger to violent death.

"When I was a child..." She stopped and swallowed the knot already forming in her throat before she continued. "When I was little, the boy who lived with his mother in our house—he drowned in the lake. I found him."

His expression softened. "That's horrible, Emmie."

She nodded slowly. "He was my friend, like Lily was yours and Angela's. And he was all... purple and bloated." She winced as the image passed through her mind. "Because I found him, the police even thought I had something to do with it."

"That's just—"

"Standard procedure? Is that what you are going to say?"

Flavio pushed his lips together then nodded and spoke softly. "That's why this touches you so much, isn't it? Because of that boy you found."

His tenderness almost broke her, but she held back her emotions. "Yes, it is. And because you're here now, I know it touches you too. I can handle anything you show me."

"I suppose I like brave women," he said with a small, sad laugh. Removing his hand from the folder, he showed her a photograph of the Davidsons' crime scene. Paul shot in the chest and Skye lying only feet away shot in the back as if she'd tried to run. "It looks like an execution."

Emmie tried not to cringe at the grisly scene in the photo. "Not a burglary, then?"

He gave a non-committal shrug, but his eyes agreed with her. Looking at the photo again, he seemed to slip back into the role of cop while discussing his conclusions. "Look at how everything is undisturbed. If a stranger had done this while seeking money, then they would have tried to find it and run, knocking stuff over as they ransacked the place. No burglar ever just shoots people point-blank like that and then walks away if they have no reason to think someone is coming. They would rummage around, at least, or steal something."

"So..."

Flavio continued, "Also, they aren't so far from the entrance, both of them, as if they'd opened the door without fear. Nothing makes it seem like Paul Davidson might've had a gun or tried to protect his home. Why would his wife be near him if he had any concerns? He would have told her to stay away while he checked out the noises. The theory was that he had his gun with him, and the stranger wrestled it away, as it wasn't found, but he never even tried to fire a shot? There aren't any signs of a scuffle here..." He pointed to the rug under the bodies, which lay undisturbed.

"It wasn't a stranger," Emmie said.

Flavio nodded. "Which would support the idea of the notes you found. That a relationship problem had something to do with it, and that Paul and Skye knew the person who came to the door. They opened the door, or he did, and Skye was just behind him, but he was immediately shot. She turned to run but didn't make it more than three steps before she was shot too."

"A crime of passion..." Emmie said softly.

"If I ever saw one," Flavio said.

"But then, what about Lily's death? The police claimed two separate crimes, with a little girl dying because her parents had locked her in the shed for punishment, and they couldn't set her free because they'd been killed."

He was silent, with one hand over the edge of the folder again as if to hold something back.

"I can handle it, Flavio. If Lily went through it, I have to see it."

With a deep sigh, Flavio produced a photo of Lily in the shed. "It's not stuff you can unsee, Emmie."

"I know." She took the photo from him, and her heart

ached at Lily's dehydrated little body lying sideways. She was exactly as her spirit appeared, skin clinging to bone as her body had lost its water, face cavernous. It was so wrong, so wrong.

Closeups showed that her nails were broken and caked with blood. She had tried to get out by any means possible, probably scratching at the door until she bled. Scratching until she was too weak to do anything.

Emmie didn't cry because this was beyond what any tears could help.

"So who could have done it?" she asked.

Flavio swallowed and met her gaze. "I've known most people here all my life. I've known them to be good people..."

"People are good until something drives them crazy," Emmie said, taking the photo of the couple again. "Don't they use a crime of passion as a defense? Someone lost it, didn't know what they were doing..."

"The thing is," Flavio said, "that pipe really couldn't have fallen. Emmie, I was there. It was secure."

"Someone pushed it," she said, "because I've been asking about the deaths."

"I was with Red the whole time," he said.

"He couldn't have done it—he saved me."

A flash of anxiety swept through Emmie at the thought of what might have happened had Red not warned her. The metal pipe could have crushed her to death beneath the rocks that it kicked up on the way toward her.

"But it's crazy," he said, running his hands through his hair. "For someone to try to kill you when all you did was read about the murders. I mean, someone has gotten away with this for years, looked everyone in the face and then gone on with their life. They stepped out of the shadows just because a visitor decided to read about it?"

"Maybe that's the problem," she said slowly. "The murderer hasn't felt threatened in such a long time but maybe the guilt has been building all these years. I come along and stir things up, meeting with a cop..."

He gave a small laugh. "If it hadn't been for the library ratting you out, they'd all just think you liked me."

They exchanged a warm glance. Looking at grisly crime scenes probably wasn't bolstering a romance, but she was grateful for Flavio—that he should be there, and that he should be a decent man, and above all, that he was too young to be "PT."

"Sherry warned me that I shouldn't go prying into this. It wasn't Red, but Angela told me he was having an affair around that time. What if it was with Skye, and Sherry found out, lost it and killed Lily's mom? Maybe she thought she would find Skye alone, but Paul was there and she had to kill him too."

Flavio grimaced as if he didn't want to hear about all his friends' bad behavior. "Sherry... God, I really love that woman."

"I know, but someone you love probably did this. And she wouldn't even need to be a great shot. I mean, this is two shots at close range. Anyone mad enough could pull the trigger and succeed."

But his eyes had narrowed as he considered this, and he shook his head. "There was no hesitation. And I highly doubt Sherry has ever killed anything before, or even shot a gun."

Emmie considered the other options, but it pained her to even think about it. She watched Flavio's reaction as she spoke cautiously. "What about Kelsey? Or Marty? Kelsey and Marty both served in the military, didn't they? So they wouldn't be strangers to killing, and it sort of looks like someone was on a mission."

"Marines..." Flavio rubbed his forehead. A little agitation passed over his face as if he were conflicted about what to do next. "Those notes that you showed me earlier... The initials?"

"PT."

He nodded for a moment, as if that rang a bell now, but a distant one. "If someone really did try to kill you this morning, then what's stopping them from finishing you off with another 'accident'? I'll look more into this, but maybe you'd be safer back home, Emmie? I could take you to the bus station. Pay your ticket if you need it."

She appreciated the gesture. He wasn't trying to get rid of her, but how could she explain that she had a commitment to the ghost of a little girl, that she needed to see this through to the end? There was a deep concern in his eyes, flowing from his experience as a cop and his kind heart, and he no doubt understood the dangers of her remaining in town better than she did.

Still, she couldn't leave. "I don't think anyone will try anything tonight, especially so soon after the other incident. It would be too obvious. The killer must have settled down after whatever I stirred up."

"The killer is impulsive." Flavio tapped one of the crime scene photos before he put it back in the folder.

"I understand, but tonight is the bonfire." She could sense Flavio's unease at her stubbornness, but what could she say to buy her more time? Lily needed her. She lied, "I'll find an excuse to leave in the morning."

He met her gaze, seemingly resigned to her decision. "If you get the slightest hint of anything unusual..."

"I'll be fine."

14

Angela and her parents hadn't yet returned when Emmie arrived back at the house. Parking her friend's car in exactly the same spot she'd found it, her mind still reeled over the photos and the discussion about the murders.

She couldn't get Lily out of her mind, and instead of entering the house, Emmie walked out to the fire pit then followed the edge of the cliff around toward the lighthouse.

"Lily, where are you?" Emmie said into the cool breeze.

The girl's presence hovered at the edge of Emmie's awareness, but sometimes the spirits didn't appear when she expected them to. She wouldn't avoid Lily's spirit anymore—there were so many questions that she longed to ask her. Maybe Lily couldn't provide any answers, but she might direct her to new clues.

Emmie was getting closer—she could feel it—but the pieces didn't quite fit together yet.

Passing the edge of the cliff where the metal pipe had nearly crossed her, Emmie kept her eyes open for anyone living or dead. She wouldn't let her guard down again. Red's truck wasn't parked in the lighthouse driveway, and Flavio had just gone back to the station. She wouldn't have much time to explore since the others would return any minute to prepare for the bonfire and barbecue that night. But without Red or Flavio around, there was nothing to stop her from taking what might be her last look around the Davidsons' land. Still, she'd be careful.

The lighthouse loomed above her as she circled around it. No sign of the girl in any of the tower windows.

"Come on, Lily," Emmie said almost in a shout, "they'll all be back soon."

The shed caught her eye. The place where Lily had died, according to both the police reports and what Angela had said.

Lily had built a fort among the wood scraps earlier. It now made sense: The girl hadn't built a fort, she had barricaded herself in. To protect herself from someone? Had her parents locked her in the shed, or had she gone there to hide from the killer?

It was the only thing Emmie couldn't connect. The parents gunned down in the house and Lily left to die alone seemed almost separate.

Emmie walked to the shed and opened the door. The hinges squeaked as it opened, and she had a sense that someone was near. A quick glance around the area revealed that she was still alone.

Stepping inside, she found a few pieces of furniture: a broken cot, a long bench seemingly taken from a picnic table, a faded rug bunched against one wall, and a wooden chair missing a leg. The shed wasn't over twenty years old, judging by its sturdy construction, but the wood had rotted away along the edges and spiderwebs filled the upper corners. No doubt, the developers would also tear it down soon and erase the memories of whatever had happened in there.

The floors squeaked as she stepped further inside. Someone had folded up the cot and leaned it against the wall. They had found Lily on it, as the crime scene photo had shown.

"Lily," Emmie said within the stillness, "you've got to tell me what happened. I'm sorry I didn't listen before, but I will now."

A sudden gust of wind blew over the shed, rattling the entire structure as if the thing might shatter and blow away at any second.

The door slammed shut.

Darkness blinded Emmie. Turning back toward the entrance with her hands outstretched, she strained to reach the door. Within a few seconds she'd found it, but it wouldn't open. Pushing and pounding her fists against it made no difference. Someone or something had locked it.

Panic welled up inside her as her heartbeat filled her ears. She gasped and prepared to scream, but hesitated. No one would hear her, and even if Angela was home, what would her friend think after finding Emmie snooping around again? At least, she had to try to get out on her own.

Pushing as hard as she could against the door, she took in a deep breath and calmed herself. Had someone locked her in? There was no sound of anyone outside, but if the person who had pushed the metal pipe down the cliff hadn't left...

A sensation in her chest swelled until she felt a presence in the darkness somewhere in front of her. An icy chill swept through the air. The familiar sensation of a spirit.

As her eyes adjusted to the slivers of light that streamed in through the cracks around her, she made out the faint details of a young girl. Lily. The girl was trembling. Her skin and clothes were soiled, just as she must have appeared when she'd died. She was hunkered in the corner of the shed with her frail fists up near her face. Her pleading eyes turned toward Emmie. Dried tears left a trail down to her chin.

The horrific scene chilled her blood and Emmie longed to reach out and comfort the girl. Hunkering down in front of her, Emmie gathered all her courage to face the tragedy.

Lily's hands were thin and wasted. The sides were bruised, probably from beating at the door. Her nails were broken and bleeding, just as the photos she'd seen with Flavio had shown. She had tried to claw her way out. The scratch marks along the edges of the door looked so fresh. If Emmie hadn't known the full story, she might have thought the shredded edges were the work of a caged animal. Flavio probably also had a photo of this but hadn't shown it. Signs of the girl's desperation were everywhere, and death hung thick in the air. The depth of the tragedy pierced Emmie's heart again and again. Lily had died alone and not far from people who could have saved her.

The girl's expression didn't change, and when she opened her mouth, nothing but a dry gasp came out. Was her parched throat too dry for her to say even a word? She had probably screamed her throat raw.

Emmie could only imagine the levels of terror and pain the girl must have endured while slowly dying alone in the shed, with her parents murdered in the house. Unimaginable violence for someone so vulnerable.

The girl sank a little further, as if moving away from the door.

"Who killed your parents?" Emmie asked. "Do you know?"

Lily didn't respond. Maybe she could communicate in some other way. A gesture or a muffled word, anything to pass along even a single clue.

Something in Lily's hand caught Emmie's attention. The girl was holding an object crumpled in her clenched fist, a silver hair clip broken in half. She must have used it to scratch at the door when her nails broke.

Lily opened her fist and let it fall to the floor. At the moment it cracked against the wood, Lily disappeared.

Emmie dug out her phone and switched on flashlight mode to light the space where Lily had sat. The spirit's icy presence had also left, but dust covered the silver hair clip, and it lay in the same place where Lily had dropped it only a moment earlier. Apparently, nobody had found it since the girl's death.

Picking it up and dusting it off, she examined it more closely. Those two rows of teeth clamped shut would never have saved the girl.

Had Lily wanted her to find it?

Slipping it into her pocket, Emmie stood up. The door was still locked, but she used the light from her phone to peer through the cracks and find the lever on the door blocking her way out. It was up high, near the top of the doorframe, far out of reach for a girl of Lily's height. She never would have made it out of the shed alone.

When she pushed the door this time, it snapped open with ease. A fluke? Either that or Lily had wanted her there with her for a moment. Maybe to show Emmie what had happened, or the girl had meant to say something with the hair clip? It was impossible to know for sure.

With a gasp of relief, Emmie stepped out into the sunshine and glanced toward Angela's house. Marty's car sat in the driveway.

15

M arty had his back toward Emmie when she walked into the house. He was putting away groceries methodically, and he didn't turn around when she entered.

"Hey," Emmie said, stopping herself from brushing any more dirt out of her clothes. "Where are the girls?"

"Went to see Kelsey's dad," he said in a monotone. "Thought they'd drop some groceries and look in on him."

"Need some help?" she asked.

Two bags of groceries sat on one counter as he unloaded another into the fridge. She stepped toward them, catching his solemn face for a moment as she dug out a loaf of bread from one bag and scanned the kitchen for where she might put it.

"I went out looking for you," he said.

"Sorry, I was out for a walk. Near the cliff. I just love watching the ocean." She walked the bread to an oversized basket that held two other nearly empty bags and placed hers inside.

He nodded, closed the refrigerator and turned to face her, leaning against the counter. "You are one brave girl."

"Am I?" She smiled curiously.

"Walking by the cliff on your own after you almost died there. Aren't you afraid of anything?"

Emmie paused while lifting a can of soup from one bag. "Mom always told me to get right back on the horse. Face your fears."

He gave a small laugh and his gaze drifted to the window, seemingly hypnotized by the view. "I also love living by the ocean. It's a luxury few can afford. The power of it draws me in and makes me feel like all the stress and worries and mistakes just *wash* away. But it's never enough."

She followed his eyes. It seemed he was staring at the pile of scrap wood instead of at the ocean. "It's beautiful up here. Doesn't seem like you have a lot to worry about."

"I was in the war," he said slowly. "And then I jumped right into the thick of things when I got out as a cop in a big city before we came here. You see stuff."

"Of course... Sorry, that was stupid of me."

"What's gotten you so attracted to that lighthouse?" he asked suddenly.

"It's fascinating." She made a concerted effort not to stammer. "Curiosity about the history, with all the talk of bootleggers."

He grinned. "Is that what it is? Moonshiners? Seems like you're more interested in its recent history?"

She opened her mouth and carefully chose her words. "I didn't mean to be nosy. It's only natural for someone to want to know what happened."

His face reddened. "You are a guest here. My daughter doesn't have to relive that. I don't have to—or my wife."

Emmie had known his mood was strange, but his sudden outburst caught her off-guard. He wasn't wrong to protect his family from more trauma, especially of the kind they had endured. Any good father would do the same thing.

"I'm sorry. I won't go back there."

He nodded. "That's good. You got all your questions answered."

An awkward moment hung in the air between them. She had outstayed her welcome and it was clear she would need to leave. Her heart ached thinking of all the terrible pain she'd stirred up for Angela's family. She had run out of time and maybe even lost Angela's friendship.

I pushed it too far. I've been so horribly selfish.

Her phone rang and she shuddered when it vibrated in her back pocket. Digging it out, she looked at the caller ID. Flavio. A mix of relief and apprehension swept through her, along with another idea. Marty would help her with an excuse to leave, she was sure of it, and maybe she could leave before Angela and Kelsey returned if Flavio could pick her up.

With Marty's gaze still fixed on her, she raised a finger and answered it. "Hi Flavio," Emmie said softly.

"Where are you now?" Flavio's tone was urgent and direct.

"I'm here at Angela's house, with Marty."

"Just you and him?"

She hesitated. "Yes."

"Speak and act natural," he said in a steady voice. "Move away from Marty, if you can."

Meeting Marty's focused stare, she smiled and raised a finger again as if she needed a little more privacy. She moved into the living room, then glanced back to make sure he hadn't followed her. He was still in the kitchen.

"What is it?" she whispered.

"The initials, PT," he said. "It's Papa Tango. I thought it'd sounded familiar. It was Marty's codename in the military."

Emmie gasped and tried to speak, but no words came out.

"Walk away slowly. Find a reason to go outside and wait for me by the driveway. I'm already on my way. Got it?"

She finally managed to speak. "Got it."

After ending the call, she turned toward the front door while returning the phone to her back pocket. Her pulse throbbed in her ears as the stark truth set in. She was in the house with a murderer.

But Marty had somehow come out of the kitchen without making a sound. He stood staring at her without emotion—and with a gun in his hand.

⚜ 16 ⚘

T he cold tension surged through Emmie's body as Marty's
      stare pierced her.

"It's not so easy to be a cop, you know," he said matter-of-
factly while looking at her up and down as if contemplating her
defenses. "But one of the best skills I've learned is how to read
people, and I can read you."

Inching back, Emmie kept her hands away from her pockets
to avoid provoking him. He wouldn't hesitate to lift the gun and
fire at the first sign of resistance from her. The back door was
just behind her, only a few steps away. If she could only get
to it...

"I can see it in your eyes that you know," he said. "You went
to see Flavio about the case, didn't you? And I know he told you
on the phone just a moment ago to not seem scared, and that
I'm a murderer. There's no hiding from the truth, is there?"

Emmie strained to take in a breath, then puffed out a single
word. "No."

"Not forever," he agreed. "I saw that look in your eyes at the
party on the first night. You saw something then, didn't you?"

She took another step back, but he shook his head as if
warning her.

"What did you see?" Marty continued. "A vision? A ghost? Did you hear their voices calling to you? Sometimes the dead just refuse to let it go and so they come back to haunt us. Don't you know that I've been haunted all these years?"

"No." She moved back suddenly and jarred her elbow against the edge of a chair. A sharp pain shot up her arm to the back of her neck and she winced.

Marty moved as well. His gun dangled at his side, and his dead eyes didn't even seem to blink. "I did a little research after you went snooping in the library. That little boy you found in the lake in Minnesota. You claimed you saw his spirit... I believe you, especially after the way you've been acting. I believe these things. Who did you see here?"

"I don't know what you're talking about."

He furrowed his brows. "Don't lie to me."

"I'm not lying."

"You are!" he screamed with wide eyes, but his outburst allowed her to stumble another two steps back without him noticing. "Don't you think I know the truth about you? A *psychic* —" He seemed to almost plead with her. "I just want to know. Did one of them talk to you? Which one?"

"I saw her," Emmie spoke softly and dared to take another step back.

"Skye?" A moment of intense anguish flashed over his face.

"Lily." She clenched her teeth to hold back a torrent of disgust. "A little girl like your own—"

"Shut up!" he screamed, covering his ears with both hands, even the hand with the pistol, and pressed his eyes shut as if to block out the truth.

This was her chance. She'd already reached the door, and her fingers fumbled around the doorknob for only a moment before she opened the door and backed outside.

He kept pace with her, only a few feet away, aiming the silver revolver straight toward her chest.

Emmie stepped into the sunshine and cool breeze. What

could she do except to keep him talking until Flavio arrived? "Why did you kill them?"

"It wasn't something I planned," Marty said.

Emmie slowed and held out her hands as if she'd given up the struggle. She listened to him—a bit of empathy to buy her some time.

"It all just happened so fast," he continued. "God knows I loved Skye—with a horrible passion. She seemed like everything to me. I'd have given up anything for her." Anguish swept over Marty's face again. "Then Skye said she wouldn't be leaving her husband like she promised, and I tried so hard to change her mind. She told me *so many times* that she didn't love him. I went there because she stopped talking to me. She wouldn't meet me anymore, so I just went there to talk, in front of him. I wanted her to admit that she didn't love him, that she loved me, and that we could be together. But when I got there, I saw them cozying up through the window. Laughing and dancing and kissing." He winced and sneered at the same time. "I just lost it."

Emmie glanced around—the first time she'd broken her eyes away from his—and calculated how far she might get before he would chase her down and shoot her. Not very far. Her only hope was to steer him toward the wood pile. Maybe she could grab a long scrap and knock the gun from his hand.

"And then," Marty continued, with tears streaming down his face, "after they were gone, I realized I hadn't truly loved Skye. I realized my family was everything to me."

The implications stunned her, and she couldn't help but lash out. "And you realized this moments after you destroyed a family?"

He stiffened as agitation swept over his face and it seemed as if his finger had touched the trigger.

Emmie tensed at the same time and snapped her mouth shut. *Keep him cool, girl. No need to provoke him.* Flavio would be there soon. But Marty's words enraged her. Was he really admitting that he might not have killed three people if he had only remembered the love for his family half an hour earlier?

She shook away the thoughts. It didn't matter. Nothing she could say would change what had happened.

His eyes filled with tears. "I realized Kelsey was the best woman in the world. A woman who had fought by my side, had my child. A woman so honest and true, worth a million times more than that lying bitch Skye who had played me for a fool. She never planned to leave her husband. His money was too important. And my sweet Angie..." He sobbed, then laughed. "She hates when I call her that, but Angie was my life. Still is. I'll do anything for her."

Emmie had reached the woodpile, but Marty seemed to have a sense of what she intended to do and motioned with the gun, steering her back toward the cliff. With nowhere else to go, she could make a run for the trail down to the shore, where she had hiked with Angela earlier. But Marty was as fit as his daughter, and he no doubt knew the terrain much better than she did.

He stared deeply into her eyes with an intensity that seemed to say only one of them would get out of there alive. "I can't let you ruin this family."

A car's engine filled the air. Flavio's squad car roared into the driveway without lights or sirens, but Marty seemed to barely notice. He only continued toward her as the anguish on his face increased.

Flavio had jumped out, and he charged toward them, aiming a gun at Marty even as Marty lowered his. "Drop the gun, Marty."

Emmie stiffened as Marty squeezed the pistol's handle. It wouldn't take him more than a second to raise it and fire. In a moment of now-or-never, Emmie burst away from Marty with all her strength and focus, then jumped behind the nearest tree.

"Stay there," Flavio said to her, now circling Marty.

Marty's posture deflated as he seemed to accept defeat.

"Put the gun down," Flavio repeated in a calmer tone. "We don't need to do this."

Marty only stared back, his eyes dead, his shoulders drooping. He glanced up toward the sky as if reflecting on his life but continued inching back toward a section of broken fencing near the edge of the cliff. "Flavio," Marty said finally, "make sure they leave my family alone after this."

"After what? Just let it go and we'll talk about it."

"I just told Emmie everything. I killed them all. I killed Skye, and Paul, and little Lily. I made sure the crime scenes didn't incriminate me. It was all and only me." He gestured toward Emmie. "Do you know she can see ghosts? Just my luck that Angela would have invited *her* here, of all people." He laughed without smiling. "What are the odds?"

"Marty, whatever happened, we can work through it."

"It's too late, Flavio. Only one way out now." Marty lifted the gun and Flavio tensed, his pistol aimed at Marty's chest.

Flavio yelled, "Put down your weapon!"

But Marty was holding the gun out by the handle with the barrel pointed at the ground. He held it as if he were holding a dead rat. "You're going to need this. It's the weapon I used to kill them." With a flick of his wrist, Marty dropped the gun, and Flavio flinched when it thudded against the grass.

Flavio held his position even as Marty continued inching back. "Don't do it."

Pausing for only a moment, Marty's face showed all his sadness before he hurled himself backwards through the fence and off the edge of the cliff.

❧ 17 ❧

Angela refused to talk to Emmie after Marty's death. No text messages, no phone calls, nothing.

That didn't come as a surprise, considering all that had happened, but the pain of losing her only close friend hit Emmie hard. Only a few days earlier, they'd excitedly raced away from the grind of college classes for a spring break full of sun and ocean.

Earlier that morning, Angela had texted Flavio to let him know she had left all of Emmie's belongings in their driveway. He had graciously picked them up within an hour.

Angela's grief at losing her father must have devastated her, and the horror of discovering he was a triple murderer must have been even worse. How could Emmie blame Angela for wishing she'd never come?

The police had asked her to stick around for a couple of days after her initial testimony, to help answer any questions they might have. Flavio had offered to let her stay at his place in the meantime, and she had accepted, although they'd slept in separate rooms. Murder, it seemed, didn't pave the way for romance. Still, they had grown close—and she didn't want to think of what might have happened to her if Flavio hadn't been there, or if he hadn't believed her. She would always be grateful to him.

Neither of them had talked about Emmie's psychic past, revealed by Marty, and that suited her just fine. Maybe Flavio had dismissed Marty's words as those of a desperate man lashing out. Or maybe he'd already looked into her but had dismissed the concept of ghosts.

Marty's words before his death came back to her. ...*I've been haunted all these years...* Had he seen the ghosts next door? Or felt them? She could only see the ghosts of children, but Lily's parents would no doubt remain there waiting for justice. Or revenge?

Papa Tango had been the army's playful reference to Marty's dancing skills. Had he danced in that cave below the lighthouse with Skye Davidson while his wife blindly worked on her garden above them?

Poor Kelsey too...

As Flavio drove into the lighthouse's lot, Emmie scanned the area for any sign of Lily. Maybe the girl had already moved on after Marty threw himself over the edge of the cliff. Justice had been done, after all. The truth had come out, although not before one last tragedy had occurred. Angela had lost a father and Kelsey a husband.

"Are you sure you want to be here?" Flavio asked.

Emmie nodded once. "It's important to me."

If Lily was still there, Emmie needed to see what difference Marty's confession and death had made to her spirit. It wasn't anything she could share with Flavio, and thankfully he didn't ask.

Climbing out of the car with Flavio, she spotted Angela's house through the trees. The blinds appeared to shift after Flavio also looked.

"Well," he said, "she knows you're here."

"I wish I could say sorry."

"Nothing to be sorry about. If it's any consolation, she doesn't want to see me either."

Red's truck was there, and he stepped out from the lighthouse a moment after they arrived carrying a piece of wood that resembled the mantle of a fireplace. Flavio removed his jacket and joined in, helping him finish loading the piece onto the truck.

Kelsey had insisted that Red remove the woodpile from their land, so he and Flavio had spent most of the time since Marty's death shuttling all the wood scraps to a new location at the far end of the lighthouse property. Nobody blamed Kelsey and Angela for wanting their privacy and a chance to mourn in peace.

The developer had also delayed the demolition of the lighthouse for another week to give Red extra time.

"This is the last of it," Red said, tapping the side of his truck.

Flavio turned back to Emmie. "I need to go into town with him to help unload it. We won't be gone long, but should you be out here alone?"

She glanced toward Angela's house. "It'll be okay. I'll stay out of sight."

"Give them their space," Red said gravely. "Don't try to approach them."

"Of course not."

He seemed satisfied with her answer, then left with Flavio.

She didn't waste any time after the truck had gone out of sight. She hurried toward the utility shed. Maybe Lily would be there, or maybe the girl had gone into the lighthouse or even down to the shoreline. Emmie just wanted so much to say goodbye and share in the girl's peace.

Pushing aside the latch on the door to the shed, she opened it quietly as if to prevent startling the girl. Within the darkness, Lily was there, hunkered in the corner, just as Emmie had seen her days earlier. The girl's emaciated face showed no signs of relief. Nothing had changed in her expression, and it caught Emmie off guard.

"Lily?" Emmie inched closer. "Don't you know Marty is gone? He confessed to the murders."

The girl seemed to cower further away, as if she were still in danger.

Emmie leaned down toward her and spoke as gently as she could. "What are you afraid of? He's gone. The man who killed you is gone. Because..."

Marty's words came back to her. *I killed them all.*

Even Lily.

He had said that before leaping over the cliff.

But... he couldn't have killed Lily. Angela had given testimony about Lily dying because of abuse. She'd died in there from neglect after Marty killed her parents. But Marty had said nothing about that.

His words came back again. *I killed them all.*

A chill swept up Emmie's spine. Why did she only think of his words now? She scanned Lily's clothes, hair, and skin. The girl's messy appearance had no doubt come from her desperate attempts to break free as the thirst and hunger had consumed her, but what kind of abuse had occurred?

Emmie stared into Lily's eyes. The girl's continued misery could only mean one thing: Marty hadn't killed Lily.

So why had Angela testified that Lily's parents had locked the girl up?

A lie? To protect her dad? Or for another purpose?

She remembered the photo she'd found in the lighthouse of the Davidson family and their happy, loving faces.

And with a start, she remembered the hair clip that Lily had made her find in that same spot. It was still in her pocket. Pulling it out, she examined it in the light of the open door. Lily hadn't needed a hair clip back then. The girl had short hair in the family photo, and even now as Lily sat there, staring back at her.

Emmie's heart pounded as she held it up while staring into

Lily's desperate eyes. "This isn't yours, is it?" Emmie already knew the answer.

Lily shook her head, then cowered further into the shadows.

"Who are you talking to?"

Emmie shuddered and spun around.

Angela stood in the doorway with a rusty metal pipe in one hand.

18

E mmie couldn't move. They stared at each other for only a moment before Angela's gaze darted to the corner of the shed where Lily sat and then back to the hair clip in Emmie's hand.

"Where did you find that?" Angela demanded.

Before Emmie could answer, her friend's expression changed as she seemed to come to the same conclusion about Lily's death only a little after Emmie had. Her friend's mouth parted as she clenched her teeth.

Angela, always in need of a clip or an elastic as she ran about, unwilling to cut her beautiful long hair...

"You just couldn't leave well enough alone." Angela jumped toward the shed's door and Emmie rushed toward it at the same time. Emmie's body crashed into it just as Angela almost closed it far enough to throw the latch shut.

"No!" Emmie screamed. Angela recoiled as Emmie thrust herself through the door and ducked at the same time. Angela swung the metal pipe toward Emmie's head and it scraped the top of her scalp, the stinging pain flaring through her brain a moment later.

Emmie lurched back and ran. A group of wide pine trees

prevented her from getting out toward the main road. The trails leading down to the shoreline were behind her, but Marty's fall over the cliff still reverberated in her memory. She wouldn't end the same way, but as her friend slowly moved toward her, that seemed like the only way out.

Emmie pleaded, holding out a hand. "Don't do anything crazy, Angela."

"Crazy? Do you know what's crazy? Knowing your father jumped off a cliff... for nothing. For a tramp!" Angela countered Emmie's every move. "That tramp drove him so crazy he couldn't think straight. It wasn't his fault."

"What did you do?"

"What I had to do."

The truth unfolded in Emmie's mind, playing out like scenes in a movie. "Lily ran away—did she come to you for help?"

"I couldn't let her tell." Angela spoke like the child she'd been nine years earlier.

"The whole story of Lily's abuse was a lie? You told everyone her parents hurt her?"

"They hurt me!" Angela shrieked. "They would have hurt my family, destroyed it."

"You locked her up? You let her suffer for days before she died—not only of thirst and hunger, but of fear? Why? Why not shoot her too?"

"My dad was too good," Angela said in a dreamy voice. "He wouldn't shoot a child, and he wouldn't let me do it, so I took care of it the only way I could."

"For God's sake, you were at home. You must have heard her screaming, begging to be let out?"

Angela cringed almost imperceptibly. "No one could hear her..." Angela shrugged. "The waves are too loud."

"Lily didn't deserve that." Emmie knew dimly that she was doing it again, screaming in the face of a killer, putting her own life in danger. But Angela had gone calm and cold. No trace of guilt on her former friend's face—unlike Marty.

"And you think *my* family deserved what happened?" Angela glanced away for the first time, looking out toward the ocean as if the answer hung somewhere above the horizon. "My parents were high school sweethearts. They would've been happy forever."

Emmie saw her chance. She surged toward the lighthouse, her legs on fire within seconds as she charged ahead, struggling for each breath. Not many places to hide inside the lighthouse, but it was a better option than if Angela forced her off the cliff. She could climb to the top of the tower to the room she had explored earlier. The metal door would hold off her friend until Red and Flavio returned.

But catching Angela off guard had only improved her odds of survival slightly. Within moments, her friend's footsteps pounded against the grass and dirt behind her, slowly gaining with every second. Emmie strained to push her body faster, but Angela had the advantage here—the daily hikes and years of athletic training. Even Emmie's shoes once more failed to grip the earth, slipping several times in the sand and condensation. Each jarring lurch forward sent a flash of pain up her spine.

Maneuvering through more trees, she nearly toppled sideways only a few yards before reaching the door to the lighthouse when her foot caught a patch of gravel. Angela wasn't so lucky, also slipping within the same patch of sand and letting out a string of curses after tumbling backwards. The metal pipe in her hand crashed against the cement sidewalk before she recovered.

Emmie glanced back at Angela as she reached the door. Angela hadn't looked away, not for a moment. Her face was red and her teeth bared, as if she intended to use them at the first opportunity. A deep sadness swept through Emmie. Her friend was gone in every sense.

Angela scrambled to her feet within seconds. "You killed my dad."

"No, Angela." Emmie rushed into the lighthouse and sprinted toward the stairs. The structure was nearly bare with both railings gone, and it was then that Emmie realized the metal pipe Angela held was one of the pieces from that same railing. The structure wobbled and squeaked as she raced up as cautiously as she could manage, steering herself away from the sides to keep from falling over the edge.

Angela entered the lighthouse before Emmie had reached the first landing, and she continued the race undeterred. Their pounding footsteps echoed through the gutted shell of a lighthouse, rattling the structure to its limit.

Was Angela shaking it on purpose?

Her friend was only a few steps behind, and twice her metal pipe caught the back of Emmie's shoe, missing her flesh by millimeters. But each blow threw Emmie off balance to the brink of tumbling over the side. And Angela relentlessly taunted her, banging the metal pipe against the structure every few steps, the deafening noise reverberating like a gunshot.

"I hate you," Angela repeated between gasps of breath.

"You can't get away, Angela," Emmie said, "Everyone will know…"

"I don't care!"

Just as Emmie reached the top of the stairs, she threw herself into the tower with a final surge of energy. Before she could even close the door behind her, a gasp and then a terrifying scream filled the air. Metal screeched and snapped as Angela clutched Emmie's shoe, ripping it from her foot as she shifted away. Her friend's face filled with terror before dropping out of sight below the tower's floor.

The deafening crash lasted for only a few seconds, and then there was silence. The dust took longer to clear, but finally Emmie could see all the way to the bottom again, where Angela lay in a bloody heap, unmoving beneath the twisted metal stairway.

19

E   mmie stared into the rising flames as Flavio tossed the last
     scraps of wood onto the bonfire. The police had delayed
the lighthouse demolition and the bonfire yet again after
Angela's death, as they photographed and studied the scene.

Now the flame's flickering warmth—cathartic, mesmerizing,
and painful at the same time—almost seemed to dance as it
spread slowly through the pile.

"It'll take a few hours to really get going," Flavio said.

Red was keeping an eye on the embers as they drifted into
the air and floated back to earth before burning out.

The demolition men hired by the developer had wasted no
time in tearing down the lighthouse. Wearing yellow vests, hard
hats and thick boots, they moved among the debris wielding
sledgehammers and jack hammers to rip away the structure's
skeleton. A crane tore away the larger sections piece by piece,
placing each part onto a massive dump truck parked next to it.

The roaring noise and clatter from all the machinery threatened to drown out their conversation, so they had moved around
to the opposite side of the bonfire with their back to the forest
as they reflected on all the violence and the grief.

Emmie glanced toward Angela's house. The windows were

dark and motionless. Kelsey had gone to live with her father, according to what Flavio had told her. The woman was strong, but she had so many horrible things to process, and it would take her a long time to recover and deal with the tragedies.

Red stepped away and toward his truck as the fire began to die out. Flavio stayed by Emmie's side.

There was still Lily. Would the girl's spirit have lingered, even after Angela's death?

"Did they tear down the shed yet?" Emmie asked.

Flavio glanced over in that direction, although it was out of sight from where they stood. "Don't think so. Probably do that last."

Stepping away from Flavio, she looked at him. "I need to do one last thing."

Flavio gave her an odd look, maybe thinking she didn't know how to leave well enough alone, not even now, but then he nodded once as if accepting that she believed in things he didn't understand. "Holler if you need anything."

"Would you hear me above the ocean?"

He nodded. "I'd be there in a heartbeat."

She believed him.

Making her way across the property toward the shed, she caught a glimpse of Angela's house again and couldn't help feeling a deep sadness for the friend who'd never really existed— a happy, carefree girl with a generous heart. Marty had destroyed the lives of so many with his selfishness, but he must have felt horror watching Angela go about life without an ounce of remorse over what she'd done to Lily, and knowing he was no better than her. Even at the very end, he'd tried to save his daughter, fully aware of her true dark nature.

If Lily was still inside the shed, maybe Emmie would need to coax her out, to help the girl see that justice had been done.

Opening the shed door, Emmie found it empty.

But a moment later she heard the girl's laughter among the trees behind it and spotted Lily lurching from tree to tree as she chased a squirrel who seemed oblivious to the spirit trying to catch it. Her face was full of joy and peace.

Lily's bright eyes met Emmie's for a second before she smiled and continued on her way through the trees until she disappeared into the shadows.

"Go find your parents now, if you can," Emmie whispered. "They're waiting for you."

Get the next book in the series now!
Hanging House: An Emmie Rose Haunted Mystery Book 1

Get the next book in the series on Amazon!
Hanging House: An Emmie Rose Haunted Mystery Book 1

AND get a **FREE** short story at my website!

Looking Glass: A Fantasy Thriller Short Story

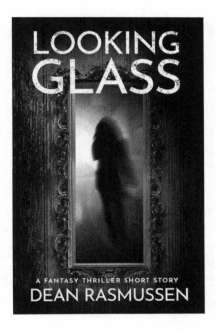

Subscribe to stay in touch!

www.deanrasmussen.com

www.amazon.com

If you liked this book and have a moment to spare, I would greatly appreciate a short review on the page where you bought it. Your help in spreading the word is *immensely* appreciated and reviews make a huge difference in helping new readers find my novels.

All FREE on Kindle Unlimited:

Hanging House: An Emmie Rose Haunted Mystery Book 1
Caine House: An Emmie Rose Haunted Mystery Book 2
Hyde House: An Emmie Rose Haunted Mystery Book 3
Whisper House: An Emmie Rose Haunted Mystery Book 4
Temper House: An Emmie Rose Haunted Mystery Book 5

Dreadful Dark Tales of Horror Book 1
Dreadful Dark Tales of Horror Book 2
Dreadful Dark Tales of Horror Book 3
Dreadful Dark Tales of Horror Book 4
Dreadful Dark Tales of Horror Book 5
Dreadful Dark Tales of Horror Book 6
Dreadful Dark Tales of Horror Complete Series

Stone Hill: Shadows Rising (Book 1)
Stone Hill: Phantoms Reborn (Book 2)
Stone Hill: Leviathan Wakes (Book 3)

ABOUT THE AUTHOR

Dean Rasmussen grew up in a small Minnesota town and began writing stories at the age of ten, driven by his fascination with the Star Wars hero's journey. He continued writing short stories and attempted a few novels through his early twenties until he stopped to focus on his computer animation ambitions. He studied English at a Minnesota college during that time.

He learned the art of computer animation and went on to work on twenty feature films, a television show, and a AAA video game as a visual effects artist over thirteen years.

Dean currently teaches animation for visual effects in Orlando, Florida. Inspired by his favorite authors, Stephen King, Ray Bradbury, Richard Matheson and H. P. Lovecraft, Dean began writing novels and short stories again in 2018 to thrill and delight a new generation of horror fans.

ACKNOWLEDGMENTS

Thank you to my wife and family who supported me, and who continue to do so, through many long hours of writing.

Thank you to my friends and relatives, some of whom have passed away, who inspired me and supported my crazy ideas. Thank you for putting up with me!

Thank you to everyone who worked with me to get this book out on time!

Thank you to all my supporters!

Made in United States
Orlando, FL
15 October 2023

37918585R00067